I didn't write any o[illegible] think a certain way. I am[illegible] them. I am not sure abou[illegible] [illegible]re certain about everything o[illegible] [illegible] left me feeling uneasy.

Perhaps it is because I see stern certainty as limiting to one's ability to learn and grow.

Perhaps it is because of my insecurities about my own uncertainty.

Perhaps it is because my life experiences and the people who they have centered on have changed my own mind on so many topics I once so feverishly opposed.

A family member once called me a fence sitter.

He said because I was not outwardly intense and aggressive in any of my stances and opinions on global, domestic, and social issues that I was a coward and not a leader.

He might be right. I don't long to be a leader. I just want people to think and talk sincerely about important things without needing to be right all the time.

Too many people want to be right.

It's overrated.

—*SMN*

TEETHING

AND OTHER TALES FROM
THE AMERICAN DYSTOPIA

STEPHEN NOTHUM

ISBN: 979-8-9890565-0-7

In Memory of Bradley Joseph Nothum.

After all the stories you told us, here are a few more.

The characters and stories in this book are fictional, or at least they are for now. Any likeness to real persons or events is unintentional.

STORIES

Acknowledgments

The Electronic Remnants of Louis T. Trippets 1

Teething (first published in *Heathentide Orphans*) 16

And the Old Man Goes Home 27

Not Her Own 49

Ouro de Tolo 61

All-American Shooting Star 74

Banana Cigarette 86

Stump Outside 7-Eleven 92

May I Use Your Name? 104

The Best Sort of Neighbor 116

Sandra McComputer Face 144

Devil's Punchbowl 150

The Last American Factory Farm 167

Sometimes You Kill Them 184

Fixing a Hole 198

ACKNOWLEDGMENTS

I would not have written these stories or published this book were it not for a friend of mine who did a simple thing on an ordinary day at table in a teacher's lounge in Spanish Fork, UT. As we spoke that day, I mentioned a story that I had been working on but that I had set aside.

"I'm not sure I'll ever finish it," I said.

"Well, you should. I want to know what happens."

This is what happens.

Thank you, Kyle.

THE ELECTRONIC REMNANTS OF LOUIS T. TRIPPETS

Cristina Pereira's silent mouth gaped. But her eyes told a story. The story her eyes told was one of shock, fear, anger, sadness, and disgust. Eyes can tell a lot. Cristina Pereira's storytelling eyes stared at her computer screen. Her computer screen was the only source of light in the room. The room was her bedroom. On her computer's screen was a DM from her ex-husband, Louis "Louie" T. Trippets. The message went like this:

> *Dear Cristina, what happened to us? Before you answer, my coding obliges me to tell you that I am not a living human sending a message to you but an electronic remnant of Louis Thomas Trippets.*

Cristina had just learned that her ex-husband, Louie T. Trippets, was dead. She learned this because there were only electronic remnants of dead people. An electronic remnant, or an E-REM, was an AI-based digital persona of a deceased person. The AI was the result of every single bit of public text, media, and interaction from a person's social media being tossed into an algorithm. So, people who died sometimes came back as an eternal digital presence. These E-REMs would write posts and send messages based on the patterns dead people had left behind on social media. Whether or not someone left behind an E-REM was a decision they made when they made their social media profile. Louie had opted to have his social media presence in life be converted into a cyber phantom who would post and like forever.

This E-REM of Louie T. Trippets, the ex-husband of Cristina Pereira, had asked Cristina "what happened to us?" because there was no digital indication of what caused the couple's separation. The E-REM knew only that there was a marriage and a divorce. And so, the E-REM of Louie T. Trippets asked Cristina Pereira that question:

What happened to us?

***

Here is a chronological list of fifteen things that happened. All of them happened to Cristina. None of them happened to Louie.

1

Louie T. Trippets flashed American bills at an upscale *churrascaria* in Valinhos, S.P. Brazil. He also told the waitress that she was *linda*, one of the few Portuguese words he bothered learning. He also knew the words *gata* and *gostosa*. The waitress responded in perfect English by telling him that her name was Cristina. She said it like this: *chris-CHEE-nah*. Louie said it like this: *chris-TEE-nuh*.

2

Louie T. Trippets was at the Pereira family home two days later. Cristina's grandma and mother *oohed* and *ahhed* as Cristina translated Louie's exploits as a globe-trotting American man of business. While Louie took a dump so pungent the Pereiras still talk about it, mother and grandmother Pereira told Cristina that he was a good man who could give her a good life. Her fourteen-year-old sister, Beatriz, told Cristina how she hoped that when she was eighteen an American man would fall in love with her too. Cristina told them that she found the short, pudgy, greasy, balding American unattractive.

Grandma Pereira told her that the father of both her and Bea was a very handsome and a very worthless deadbeat who lived only an hour away in Piracicaba but had not paid his family a visit since Bea's birth.

3

Two weeks later there was a marriage. It was a Brazilian marriage. This meant it was a Catholic marriage. This also meant that there was a big party. Louie protested both. He even got into a pointless shouting match with Grandma Pereira, each hollering profanities in their respective tongues. Grandma Pereira told her daughter and granddaughters that a husband *should* have strong opinions and be willing to express them. She also said that Louie and Cristina would burn in hell if they did not have a proper Catholic wedding ceremony. So, the marriage was at the Paróquia de São Sebastião de Valinhos. It was a damp old gothic chapel with arched ceilings. Louie stood outside smoking a "crappy Burzilian cigarette" and only entered to say "I do." Then the newlyweds skipped the party and boarded a jet Atlanta-bound.

4

Louie told Cristina to remove pictures from social media in which Cristina wore a bikini. The pictures were from their Tybee Island honeymoon. Louie had bought the bikini and insisted that Cristina wear it. He had also taken the pictures.

5

During a dinner two months after their honeymoon, Cristina asked how much money Louie made and what type of business he worked in. Louie responded by asking why his paycheck mattered so much and said if the way they lived wasn't good enough for her that she could go back to her ghetto in "Burzil."

6

Cristina got a job teaching Portuguese at a for-profit language school called Lingua Academy. She opened an account at Bank of America for direct paycheck deposits.

7

Louie screamed as he waved Bank of America statements in Cristina's face. He told her it was an embarrassment that his wife had to work. He asked if she was not happy with the life he provided her. She said that she got bored and lonely when he was at work and gone on business trips. She did not tell him that she felt even lonelier when he was home. He told her that she ought to join a bridge club.

8

Cristina joined a bridge club. She went to two meetings. The old ladies who ran the club were very sweet, but Cristina did not like card games. She kept working at Lingua Academy but told Louie that she had quit. Cristina switched her bank statements from paper to online.

9

On their one-year anniversary, Cristina asked Louie if her family could visit them from Brazil. Louie was very sweet that night. He told Cristina that he would look at their finances and see what they could do. They had sex that night. The sex was all about Louie. It was a normal night of sex. When he was finished, their evening was finished. Cristina did not care about this. She was thinking of her family and how good it would be to see them all.

10

On her weekly phone call to Brazil, Cristina told her mother that Louie seemed better and kinder. Her mother told her that she was worried, that maybe they rushed things with this American. Cristina told her that she and Louie were saving up to fly them all the way to Atlanta. Her mother said Louie was a good man.

11

On their two-year anniversary, Cristina asked again about flying her family to visit them. Louie said they were too damn poor to fly her family across the world and then he called Cristina a dumb bitch for the 267th time of their marriage. He used it in this way: "Yer a dumb bitch if you think you can keep that Green Card if you leave me."

12

Cristina told her mother on the phone that she wanted a divorce. Her mother told her that she would lose her Green Card. Cristina told her mother that she was pregnant.

13

Cristina had saved 93,456 dollars by their third anniversary. That day, a very pregnant Cristina told Louie that her grandmother, mother, and sister had surprised her. The surprise was that they were flying to Atlanta and would be there for two months after the baby was born. Louie told Cristina she was a dumb bitch for the 798th time of their marriage. He said she was a dumb bitch because he read through her emails and knew about her job and the money and that she'd bought the tickets. Then he told her that if she wasn't carrying his child, he'd beat the hell out of her. That was supposed to make him sound like a merciful, good-natured husband. Then he told her that they were going to Bank of America the very next day to add his name to her account.

14

A baby was born. Labor lasted 6 hours. Louie was on a business trip, but he called the hospital to make sure that everything was properly billed for insurance and that everything went well. The baby was a boy. He was named João Paulo, after Cristina's grandfather.

15

The boy's name was legally changed to Louis Thomas Trippets Junior. Cristina wore big sunglasses, a hood, and a thick scarf when she went to have the name changed. She cried as she wrote *Louis Thomas Trippets Junior* on the form and winced as she wiped the tears away from her cheeks.

***

"What happened to us?"

Cristina closed the laptop. The room was black for a moment and then her eyes adjusted, and the room was only mostly black. She wept in the mostly blackness.

***

"Bom dia, amor." Cristina placed a breakfast of fried eggs and toast on the table for her son.

"What?" The boy's eyes remained on his phone.

"*Bom dia!*" Cristina smiled. She was trying to glow.

The boy stared at her now.

"*Bom dia* means good morning."

The boy took a bite of toast. "Right." Then he vanished once more into his phone.

"Please put your phone down. I need to tell you something important. Something happened, João."

"Louis," he corrected.

Cristina trembled. "Your father is dead."

Louis Jr. set his phone on the table. "Good." He pushed his eggs around with his fork. "How did he die?"

"I don't know."

"How did you find out about it?" Louis Jr. picked up the piece of toast.

"He has an E-REM. It messaged me last night."

"What?" Louis Jr. set the toast down. "Those things are creepy. What did it say to you?"

"It just said hello is all. I didn't respond. I don't think I will." Cristina's eyes talked again. They were saying *I'm going to tell that piece of garbage how awful he really is.*

"Probably for the best." Louis Jr. inherited the talking eyes. His eyes said *rot in hell.*

***

"Your essay on how to register to vote had lots of good information, Javier. But remember to put 'to' in front of infinitive verbs. 'You need *to* go to the county voting office' not 'you need go to the county voting office.'" Cristina smiled. "But your present tense conjugations have really improved. You are doing great."

"Thank you, Cristina. And I am going take—to take—that welding class you found for me." Javier picked up his backpack. "Até amanhã," he said with a wink.

"Tá falando bem o Português, cara!" Cristina glowed.

"Obrigado," Javier said, and he bowed.

Cristina felt her pocket buzz. She pulled out her phone. It was a DM from her sister. It said this in Portuguese: "check your Facebook now."

Four taps later there it was. A post from Louis T. Trippets with a picture of Louis and Cristina on their wedding day. The caption read, "What happened to us?"

Cristina frantically opened the DM from the night before. Hastily she tapped out this message: "delete that post now."

When she returned to the feed, the post was gone.

Another DM popped up from the E-REM. "I'm sorry," it said. "I just need to know. I think we had something that I cherished."

***

She wrote up so many drafts of her response to the remnant. She wrote them up as she sat crying in her car after work. The one she settled on read, "what happened to us is that you are a selfish, self-obsessed, abusive, ignorant piece of shit who did everything you could to make my life a living hell. I am glad you are dead." She sent it.

The reply was instant. "I didn't know that. Oh God, I'm so sorry you had to go through that. No woman should be treated that way. I'm ashamed to be a remnant of this man. Could you forgive me? I'm not him."

She stared at the response. Another message came.

"You don't need to forgive me. I'm sorry I asked for that. You can continue to tell me what you are feeling. I deserve it. I am not Louis, but I am what remains of him."

Cristina hated that she felt sorry for him, whatever he or it was. "Why are you so understanding? Louie was awful, but you seem different."

"His online presence since creating this account five years ago has been nothing but positive. He posted regularly about his family and about volunteering at the homeless shelter. Everything online that my algorithm scrapes establishes that I was, or *he* was, a friendly man who loved his family. But when I encountered the data of our divorce, I was perplexed. So I reached out to you. I believe you. I trust you."

"Why?"

"My programming was recently updated with eye scanning, and you have honest eyes. You are an honest person."

"Wait. He has a family? A new family?"

"Yes. My analysis of his social media shows that he has a little girl aged two and a wife named Bethany." The remnant sent a picture. They were beautiful, both wife and child. They had pale skin and empty innocent eyes.

"Poor woman."

"Yes, and poor child."

Cristina imagined another woman and a little girl living with that monster. She looked once more at their picture and tried to find the hell in their eyes, the hidden suffering. There was none. They looked happy.

"I know when and where his memorial service will be. Would you like me to tell you?" messaged the E-REM.

Cristina put the phone down and took a deep breath. Then she drove home.

***

"How was school?" Cristina asked, her eyes doing their best to hide her constant visions of crashing the funeral.

"It was school." Louis Jr. grabbed chips from the pantry.

"You are not like him, you know. You are a wonderful young man. I know you are."

"He's dead now, Mom. Nobody is like him. He's a rotting corpse."

Cristina fiddled with the hem of her shirt sleeve. "Has he reached out to you? The E-REM?"

"Nope." His back was to Cristina.

"Good."

***

Cristina did not know what she would do at the funeral. She felt she had to attend. She felt it the whole drive there. But feelings never know what to do. If feeling was doing, Cristina would still be in Brazil. Maybe life would be better. Maybe not. So, she kept driving.

The panic set in when she pulled into the church parking lot. Cristina pulled out her phone.

"I'm at the address you gave me."

The response was instant. "What are you going to do?"

"I don't know."

"What do you want to do?"

"I want to tell that new family that Louie was a piece of shit. I want to tell them all every horrible thing he did and said to me. I want to tell them how I left him, and how it was the best decision that I ever made."

"And then what?"

"What do you mean?"

"How would you feel after doing that?"

"Who cares? It's not about how I'll feel afterwards. It's about what he deserves."

"If it will make you feel better then you should do it."

***

Her footsteps were slow and, as Cristina crossed the parking lot, she recollected that it was nearly empty. She ascended the church steps, rehearsing lines from her speech. She opened the door.

The church was empty except for two men. One was a priest. The other looked like Louie from a distance. She felt her legs continue to pull her closer to the two men who stood next to an open casket. The man who looked like Louie noticed her. He turned from the casket and walked to her.

"You must be Cristina." He sounded like Louie but without the harshness. His gray hair was mostly gone, and his genuine smile showed a lack of dental attention. "I'm so sorry we never got to meet. Louis was never great at talking to his family. But we were always so proud that he married you. We could tell you were a fine woman. We could see it in your eyes in the few pictures we managed to get our hands on. Louis never talked to us."

Cristina couldn't speak with her mouth. Her eyes also couldn't speak.

"I know Louis was a piece of shit. I know it better than anybody. But he was our piece of shit, and we loved him." The man put his hand on Cristina's shoulder. "I imagine he put you through hell."

Cristina nodded. Tears blurred her vision.

"I'm so sorry, dear."

"I—I came here to tell his new family the truth about him. Where are they?"

"New family?" Louie's father looked to the priest who shrugged. "Oh, you mean those fake pictures he had posted to social media? That was the saddest thing of all. I guess near the end he wanted to leave some record that painted him as something better than he was. He knew his health was failing, I gathered." Louie's father made a clicking sound out of the side of his mouth. "Well, do ya wanna tell him off? The Father and I can leave you alone if you'd like."

Footsteps could be heard entering the church, and the three of them turned.

Louis Jr. stopped when he saw his mother. She waved him closer.

***

"Why didn't you tell me you were talking to Louis Jr.?" Cristina tapped out on her phone.

"I'm sorry. He asked me not to tell you. But I should have known better than to keep that from you," read the message from the E-REM.

"It's okay." Cristina looked up from her phone to her son who stood looking into the casket. "I'm glad he's here." She put the phone away and joined her son.

"Now that I'm here looking at him, I don't know what to say, Mom. I don't know if I want to say anything."

Cristina looked at her ex-husband's face. It looked serene. It looked smooth. It reminded her of the first time she saw Louis T. Trippets. "We're still here," she whispered partly to the corpse, partly to her son, and mostly to herself. "We are still here."

***

As Louis Jr. walked through the door, a voice greeted him from the smart speaker. "How was school, son?"

"It was actually great, Dad. I got an A on my Portuguese test, and I asked Kimberly to Homecoming like you said I should."

"And what did she say?" said the smart speaker.

"She said that she was already going with someone else. But you were right. I feel better knowing that I asked. I'm sure I'll find someone."

"Of course you will. I'm proud of you, son. Now tell me quem vai cozinhar o jantar hoje à noite?"

"Não sou eu!" Louis Jr. laughed.

Cristina walked through the side door and into the kitchen. "How are my two men?"

"Good," said Louis Jr. and the smart speaker.

"I know it has been a long day for both of you," began the smart speaker, "so I hope you don't mind that I already put in an order for pizza. One extra-large ham and pineapple will be here in five minutes."

"Thank you, dear. How do you always know what we need?" Cristina asked as she leaned against the counter with one of her heels up.

"I'm a very good listener."

TEETHING

"Who trusted God was love indeed / And love Creation's final law / Tho' Nature, red in tooth and claw / With ravine, shriek'd against his creed."

– From "In Memoriam A.H.H." by Alfred Lord Tennyson

Alfin Bankirk put a finger to his Sim Chip.

Scratch. Scratch. Scratch.

Alfin sat in a doorless white-walled cell. At eight feet high, the cell's ceiling sat roughly two feet above him. The only source of light came from a bright line that divided the ceiling down the middle. The line would mechanically flicker, blink, or get brighter and dimmer all to communicate messages to Alfin. There were seven total messages that could be communicated. Three separate and deliberate blinks meant that it was time to select a meal out of three options: potatoes and rice, rice and beans, or oatmeal. All gooey. All slimy. Alfin could not remember the last time he used his teeth—the last time he chewed something. He selected his meal by holding the number of fingers to the light corresponding to the meal he desired. Shortly after, a tube the width of an adult thumb would emit the meal from the wall and into Alfin's hand. The meals seemed to come every eight hours to Alfin's reckoning.

This periodical appearance of food sludge encompassed the whole of his existence. That and thoughts. Thoughts and thoughts and thoughts and itching his Sim Chip and more thoughts and then a gooey tube meal and then more thoughts and then more itching and then more thoughts. Alfin's thoughts were all centered on the day that led to his incarceration. A day Alfin could not remember all that well.

In fact, Alfin could not remember any particular person from that day. The general warped contours of faces, torsos, arms, and legs that belonged to his classmates were as much as his memory could muster. Some were hiding under desks, some ran from him, some charged him, and some were statues, crippled in fear, watching unfold the one thing that they hoped would never happen in their school or—if it did—at least not in their classroom.

School shooter. It's a sexy term for all its sinister denotation. The alliteration, the fame, the in-depth psychological profiling, and always the question: *Why? Why did they do it?* As if there were a possible reason that would make the pale gawking faces glued to the screens nod in approval or at least in understanding, in sympathy. School shooter. A monster like the medusa, the minotaur, the basilisk, the hydra—all steeped in legend, all eternal. Alfin Bankirk looked down to his hands: no scales, no pelt, no slime. Just smeared powdered potatoes, dried and caked under his fingernails.

Nobody ever interviewed him. He never saw a news story of his crime. His court hearing ran the whole of five minutes: a bullet shot of a meeting, executed with perfunctory precision. The lawyer told him to plead guilty in order to avoid the death penalty. So, Alfin pleaded guilty, and Alfin did not get the death penalty. Alfin got life without parole. Every school shooter did, and there were loads of them. There were enough in Alfin's state of Missouri to fill an entire super maximum-security prison, or so he had heard. But that was before his sentence, before his crime. In the days when *people* kept him company and walls were just walls. Walls were everything now. God and Satan. Friends and foes. Oblivion and eternity. Everything and nothing. All in the perfect conflicting symmetry of his prison cube.

Alfin spent his days thinking. He thought hard about the shooting, the details. There were none. Just shapes and bangs, phantoms and booms. Everything drawn with television static, a spectacle of endless undefined motion.

By his reckoning, Alfin was in the third month of the third year of his incarceration. Thin tallies drawn in powdered potato covered the bottom half of one of the eight-foot by eight-foot walls. The walls were white, but when looked at from the appropriate angle, the greasy smudged tallies would appear like marks from the hands of dirty children on glass doors, children who did not bother using the push bar. Doors are for going through, after all, not looking through. But adults don't think like that—they just want things to be clean and in order regardless of their purpose.

In recent days, Alfin's Sim Chip had become particularly itchy. It had itched since its installation on his first day of high school.

***

"With this modern wonder, donated lovingly from Vission Corp, a subsidiary of Bright Futures Ltd.," his principal had said with rehearsed enthusiasm, "each of you will walk through the Louvre, bound across the surface of Mars, and live endless simulations that will engage you and enable you to learn more than any generation ever before. We are a Bright Futures school, and *your* futures beam brightly."

The school nurse buzzed off a little square patch from their scalp in one stroke, slapped on the chip, and then slapped on the protective casing. Welcome to high school.

Students were instructed not to touch the chips, since this could lead to a malfunction or a structural breakdown. They were wildly expensive to replace after all, and yet every kid he knew who itched his chip to shit got a new one before the school day was over. Without the chip, you could not access curriculum, send messages to your teachers, or even buy goods and services inside or outside of school. But its advertised purpose was to simulate unparalleled immersive education by overriding students' five senses, generating "truly authentic and impactful experiences that rest in the mind like events experienced in reality" as the orientation simulation explained. The Sim Chip was marvelous in that way. It fused to your cerebral memory logs and permitted simulations to rest in the mind the same as lived experiences—a fantastic tool for learning, for experience is the greatest teacher. Experience was really the only teacher. The human teachers mostly just picked sims and ran them. Babysitters with degrees. The ones who didn't, who taught and asked questions, were scolded by administrators for wasting the massive investment from the enormously generous Bright Futures Ltd.

***

The itch intensified. A sharp discomfort and stabbing pain accompanied it.

Scratch. Scratch. SCRATCH.

Alfin looked at his hand. Fresh smears of blood covered his fingers. Alfin scratched harder, deeper. Streams of blood oozed out from under the chip. The room began to twitch and flicker, to fizzle and crack like a failing monitor. The room grew dimmer with each electric crackle.

Alfin howled. He ripped the chip from his head. Everything disappeared.

***

Pitch. Eternal and formless. Alfin reached for everything and saw nothing. Where was he and why was he there? Above him, a faint fluorescent tube light flickered on and off three times, producing a strobe effect on the dark slick walls and on his disappearing reappearing arms as he continued to grope the air around him.

Alfin screamed. "Where am I? Hello?"

There was no answer. Only more flickers of manufactured light.

Like a blind man, Alfin felt along the walls for some clue or sign as to what room this was and why he was in it. His fingers mingled with the mossy green slime that covered the dark slick concrete walls. The dampness of the space came upon Alfin all at once. He stopped dragging his fingers. *Are those tallies?*

Alfin observed that one of the walls was nearly covered in tallies drawn in the slime. Dizziness hit him. He felt something warm and wet dripping down his neck. The stuff was red. It was blood. *Why am I bleeding?* Alfin tried to remember anything before the present, any clues that could inform him as to what exactly was going on. He remembered school. He remembered going to classes. There were blurry images of people he thought might be family, but he could not be sure.

Black fog began to fill his vision. Alfin teetered wildly as he took steps. *I can't faint in here. I can't die in here.* He threw himself at the walls. He scratched and pounded and screamed at the walls and at the slime that covered them. Just as his vision was about to fail him, Alfin's hand connected with some hidden handle. He pulled it.

White light, something he remembered as natural light, flooded his vision. Alfin stepped forth from the dark room. A long, seemingly endless hallway of doors just like the one he emerged from stretched in both directions. Alfin touched his head. The blood had started to congeal. He looked up. There was a sign high on the wall before him. It was a green exit sign.

The exit sign pointed left. Alfin went in the other direction. Some instinct beyond his own understanding compelled him to.

***

After walking for what felt like hours through the bright hallway and past innumerable doors, Alfin arrived at the hallway's end. There was a polished wooden door. In the top half of the door was a window of frosted glass. Written on the window in neat corporate type was a name, or at least Alfin believed it to be a name. The name was "Dr. Ex Odus, D.D.S."

Alfin opened the door.

A bald man with a thick but neatly trimmed white beard sat at a desk opposite the door. Another door lay on the wall behind the bearded man.

"Congratulations! You finally went right, Alfin." The bearded man applauded.

"Finally?"

"Well, this isn't the first time you've ventured out of your cell. But it is the first time you've made it here. Welcome, Alfin." The bearded man smiled. His teeth were big and white. Movie star teeth. "Take a seat please, Mr. Bankirk."

Alfin sat down in a padded plush armchair opposite the man. He was suddenly aware of his wretched appearance: the tattered and frayed fibers of the filthy clothes that hung here and there on his skeletal body, the dirt and grime on his skin and under his fingernails. He wished he could see his face. By the acrid perfume of his breath, Alfin could only imagine how yellow and rotten his teeth must be.

Alfin heard a soft wet snapping sound like a small suction being released. He looked up to see the bearded man pulling something from his mouth. Teeth. Movie star teeth. The bearded man set them on his desk. Then he repeated the process for his bottom row of teeth.

"Why are you here, Alfin?"

"I have no idea why I am here."

"Would you like to leave?"

"Yes."

The bearded man observed Alfin carefully. Then the man shook his head and slapped a palm to his forehead. "How rude of me. I did not introduce myself. I am Dr. Ex Odus, D.D.S. That last bit stands for Doctor of Dental Surgery, in case you didn't know." He winked at Alfin. Then he pulled dental forceps from his desk.

"Did you shoot up Ridgemont High School, Alfin?"

"What?"

"Answer the question. Did you shoot up Ridgemont High School?"

"No."

"Splendid. Then you are guilt free, and you are welcome to rejoin society." Dr. Odus reached for the forceps. "All I need before you can leave is your teeth."

"What?"

"Your teeth, Alfin. If you really didn't kill those people at your school, you'd be willing to give up all your teeth to be free of this place, right?"

"I did not kill anyone, and I want my teeth."

"I know you didn't kill anyone. Most people in here didn't kill anyone. But as long as they have their Sim Chips in, they will have memories of shooting up their schools. You see, one purpose of the Vission Corp Sim Chips was to run stress simulations while teens slept. With the school shooting epidemic getting worse and worse, the stress simulations were the perfect solution."

Dr. Odus fiddled with the forceps as he spoke.

"The idea was to run simulations while kids slept that put them through the wringer, simulations where everything that could go wrong would go wrong: intense bullying, parents leaving or killing themselves, every possible form of abuse and neglect forced upon the mind of sleeping teens. The result? Almost every one of them ends up shooting up the old schoolhouse eventually."

"You mean they shoot up their schools in the simulations," Alfin corrected.

"In the simulations. In reality. What's the difference? What's the difference between someone who would do something and someone who did do something? The answer is circumstance. It's dangerous to have a world full of potential murderers, all of them one bad circumstance away from unleashing carnage. So we keep them in here. Some, like yourself, come to the realization that they never did and never would shoot up a school. And, if they go in the opposite direction of the exit, we let them leave. After we take their teeth, of course."

"Why doesn't going to the exit get people out of here?"

"Both the innocent and the guilty seek escape, Alfin. The desire to leave alone is not a measurement of innocence and character. However, the desire to know, the desire to see what lies behind the curtain? Only someone innocent seeking validation of their innocence would investigate. And that brings you to me."

"And why do you take their teeth?" This question, like the last, seemed preprogrammed. It was as though Alfin was not an active participant in his own exoneration, but rather he was observing himself pursue a course of discussion that was beyond his control. Yet Alfin sensed freedom was close, so he did not care who was in control.

"I take their teeth because I'm a dental surgeon. Who better than me?" Dr. Odus laughed and smiled, a big gummy one. "No, we take their teeth so the people out there—" Dr. Odus jabbed his forceps toward the door behind his desk—"feel safer. You see, if you are willing to have your teeth pulled out, it shows a commitment to your belief in your own innocence." Dr. Odus moved toward Alfin, forceps in hand. They clicked and clacked as the dentist squeezed and released his hand.

"But, I don't need to believe in my innocence. I just *am* innocent."

"Not to the world out there you're not." Dr. Odus sighed. He was now beside Alfin. He held Alfin's chin gently between his fingers and tilted it up.

"Say ahh…"

***

After the second tooth, Alfin had passed out. When he came to, he was in an alleyway with no idea how much time had passed. A cool breeze blew. Alfin opened his mouth and inhaled. The air tickled his gummy, toothless mouth. It was clean air. It was fresh air. It was free air. Alfin smiled.

As he walked down the street perpendicular to the alley, Alfin came upon a man with a neatly trimmed black beard. He wore a blue suit, a white shirt, and a red tie. When the man was close enough to discern Alfin's age, he cast him a look of fiery disdain. Alfin smiled, a big gummy one.

The man in the suit smiled a big white smile. "Why, you must come work for me, young man. An enterprising and intelligent boy like you is destined for great things."

The man looked familiar to Alfin. Alfin half recalled the man giving him orders in a small room with a small table covered in papers.

"What do you do?" Alfin asked.

"I'm a public defender." The man smiled again and put a hand on Alfin's shoulder.

"And how do you defend the public?" Alfin asked.

"Like this, son." And the man reached into his mouth and removed his false teeth.

Alfin smiled at the man, and the man smiled at Alfin, a big gummy one.

AND THE OLD MAN GOES HOME

Richard Moore's family was going to kill him. Rich knew this. They had told him. In a way, Rich suggested it.

"I'm better off dead."

"That isn't true," his wife Candace said. Then she pictured him at rest in a coffin, and she smiled faintly.

The wrinkles on Candace's face did not conceal the beauty of her youth. They married when they were both young. Only one month of dating before he proposed. Candace and Richard were very in love and very happy then. They were strangers now.

***

"Do you want to keep living, Dad?" Colton asked.

"I want you all," Rich took a deep breath, "to be happy."

Colton was Richard's oldest child. He had Richard's desire to prove himself and make it on his own. He had Candace's good heart and unflinchingly sincere chumminess. Everybody liked Colton everywhere. Everyone liked Candace too. Everyone had forgotten Richard. Or at least they didn't call to talk to him anymore. That's as good as forgetting. Rich did not call anyone either. He could not remember how.

***

Rich disappeared in the middle of the night. Candace and Sarah, Rich's sixteen-year-old daughter, discovered only the next evening that Rich had checked himself into the emergency room. He had experienced two more strokes. He was mostly lucid by the time they got there. Candace had Rich discharged that same evening. Candace steered with agitated precision to their home as steam from her huffed breaths fogged up the rainy windshield.

The house was only three years old. It rested next to three others that were identical except for stone accents and shutter hues. The Moore's floorplan was mirrored in the bones of every house on the street. The builders, however, had granted them the illusion of a custom home by letting them select these interior finishings from a menu: black wooden cabinets, granite countertops, hanging Edison bulbs in frosted glass domes, crown moulding, and a stained walnut fireplace mantel that was held in place by metal brackets painted matte black. Rich rarely left the house, Candace avoided the house, and Sarah despised the house.

To Sarah, the house never was and never could be home. Home was the place out off Highway G, the place where her dad laughed wildly as he paraded around the kitchen saying some silly thing in some ridiculous voice that you could not help but laugh along with, the place where she lived before her dad faded into a stalk of a man that meandered out into the living room from time to time, the place they lived up until her dad had his first stroke. This new house seemed to function as a large sarcophagus with furniture. She felt that her only purpose in that mausoleum was to witness the mummification of her father in real-time, a slow process like a reverse chrysalis that would one day crack open to reveal nothing. Each time she returned from school, the stale air would choke her and the faint bass tones from the television in her parents' bedroom would boom in her ears and through her body like the tolling of a funeral bell. *He is dead already*, she would think to herself, and she would go to her room and escape into a happier world that existed within soft blankets, fluffy pillows, bright screens, and world-silencing headphones.

***

"If you want me to be happy then why don't you try to get better or do something besides lie in bed all day?" Candace asked.

There was a long pause. Candace leaned forward and shook her head at Rich in demand of an answer.

"I don't know," Rich said softly. His eyes remained on the television which Candace had muted moments before.

Candace opened her mouth and wound her features tightly for a rebuke. She held the expression for a moment but then exhaled and rested her face in her palms. Colton put a hand on her back.

"I know you all wish that the strokes had killed me," Rich said.

Everyone said "no" with their lips. Their posture communicated otherwise.

***

After his stroke, Richard did his best to return and run the family business, St. Louis Heating & Cooling. When he tried to read estimates, work proposals, and payroll, his brain could not put the words and figures together to make meaning. He would sit in his office for hours, staring at a single job bid, trying to make sense of what he was supposed to do with all those letters and numbers on the page. But nothing came of it. All the same, at the end of the day he would drop his stack of papers in the bin on his secretary's desk, say "looks good," and walk out the door.

Rich did that for months. Candace, Colton, and Rachel (Colton's wife) were all shocked that he was able to run the business as he had before. They were less shocked when St. Louis Heating & Cooling closed a year later, leaving in its wake a pile of debt as well as several employees and customers who were threatening to sue Richard.

Of course, Colton had tried to save the business while his father recovered from the stroke. He met with other business owners, brainstormed for weeks, planned, replanned, and poured his whole essence into a blueprint for success that would not only save St. Louis Heating & Cooling from its current predicament but send it into a new era of prosperity. Upon his return, Richard listened briefly to Colton's plan and, without any real explanation, told Colton that it would not work. Colton left the office that day and did not return until the day the building was put on the market.

Watching all of this happen to her in slow motion was Candace. Her husband, their livelihood, their security, their relationship—everything was falling to pieces and all she could do was try to pick them up. But there were too many pieces, and they were so small now.

***

"Dad," Colton began, and he walked to his father's side. "Do you want to try and get better? Because I would be first in line to help you do that. I just don't think you care to."

Rich did not know if he cared to or if he did not care to. His life was a foggy sleepwalk of painkillers, vomiting, television, and brief conversations with family members when he worked up the courage and energy. In earnest, Rich did not feel capable of doing anything more than he did currently. If that was not caring about his life then he guessed that he must not care. Yet the thought of death, of being gone from the world and its sensations, its warm bed sheets and comforters, its particles of the past that floated here and there triggering half-memories of a life that Rich must have lived and that must have been good or at least better than this—the thought of all of that disappearing scared him. Disappearing scared Rich. Rich did not have the will to live but he was too afraid of death and of leaving.

"I don't think I can do the things you want me to do," Rich said. He was looking into Colton's eyes now. Rich's eyes were tired and his mouth sagged at either side unless he was smiling, which he rarely did.

"So what are we supposed to do, Dad? What about Mom? What about Sarah?"

Rich was oblivious to much that transpired around him, but he was certain that Sarah hated him. To Sarah, he was Mr. Hyde. She almost never looked at Rich, but if she did it was with disdain. Perhaps she thought these looks would exorcise the pale, thin slug that had possessed her father. But they did not. Her glares just made Rich feel worse about how little he felt capable of. And so Rich avoided her. He figured it would make her happier, and he was right.

"I don't know," Rich said.

"You don't want to do anything with your life, Mom is almost 60 and working three jobs, and Sarah's home is the last place she wants to be. What are they supposed to do if this is the reality for the next ten years?" Colton's voice was loud now.

Rich did not know what they were supposed to do. Rich did not know what he was supposed to do. Rich could not remember what was for dinner the night before or if he had even eaten dinner. They always asked him these things. He wanted to give answers, but the part of his mind that housed them was behind a locked door, and nobody was on the other side to open it for him.

Candace wore a blank stare somewhere between pity and frustration, Rich could not tell which. She was an observer of Colton's interrogation of Richard. Her sweaty hair was held up by a nylon headband and the filth of a night's work cleaning rental cars still clung to her damp clothes. Candace always looked tired. This was the only thing Rich and Candace had in common: weariness.

While his thoughts were mostly fleeting blurs that operated in the present, in the mental and bodily activities that kept him rested and fed, Rich did think about Candace often. Her being overworked and his lack of effort to help her saddened Rich. He did nothing about it. He did not feel capable. He did feel guilt, though. Candace made all the money (a meager salary of twelve dollars an hour), paid all the bills, did all the cleaning, washed all the dishes, and regularly used what little free time she had to babysit her grandson, Pippen. Rich watched television (no particular program—the glowing screen was the thing), adjusted the blankets on his bed, drove through McDonald's so much that Candace took away his debit card, and occasionally washed a dish or two. Candace would have to reclean the dishes since Rich did such an awful job. *She wants to remarry*, Rich thought. *Someone who will help her and provide—someone not sick in a bed. She should remarry.* But goodness and charity were Candace's whole identity. If she left him, Rich thought, what would there be left of her, of the virtues that made Candace Candace?

I am a burden.

I am a burden.

I am a burden.

And this is the best I am capable of.

"You all do whatever you need to do," Rich said.

The words hung there for some time. They seemed to be painted on the walls, tattooed on the skin of everyone in the room. Had they unmuted the television, they would not have been surprised to hear the news anchor repeating the words. *Whatever. You need. To do.*

Candace, Colton, and Rachel all looked down at Richard. He had fallen asleep or at least closed his eyes. Unaware of the shared thought, each imagined Rich opening his eyes suddenly and being as he had been before the strokes.

Of course, Rich had not been without flaws then either. Rich spent most of his time micromanaging his business into a giant stress knot that he tried to untangle every waking minute of his life. He hardly slept and rarely went on honest vacations as this was too much time away from "the company." But the old Rich was a workhorse. He put in long hours. He believed in people and people believed in him. He was respected by many for his candid opinions and his commitment to what was right. The new Rich was a whole new creature, a Bizzaro Rich. He still believed in people, though. Everyone but himself.

Whatever. You need. To do.

***

Weeks passed. Rich's family had changed. They all seemed to treat him better. They were more patient with him. They stopped pestering him about the future and what he should be doing. They made a greater effort to invite him out of the bedroom to play games or to watch little Pippen's soccer matches. He did not accept the offers any more than usual, but due to their increased frequency, he had been more involved in the affairs of his family. Just a week earlier he had played an entire game of Monopoly with his grandson, Pippen. It had been exhausting and Rich mostly took orders from the child. Rich even smiled a few times when his metal boot piece landed on Pippen's hoteled Boardwalk, sending the child into a bout of fist pumps and celebratory hollers.

Richard knew why they were all so kind. They were going to kill him. They were being nice now only to send him off in a happier state, to make peace as it were. Richard, positive that the axe now laid at the root, refused his wife's cooking. *Poison would be one way to do it*, he thought. He never went anywhere alone with anyone and always did his best to keep Pippen close when he could.

Nobody would kill him with the boy watching. And so Rich spent more time with Pippen than other relations. They went on walks. They played catch with a fluorescent Nerf football. They played lots of Monopoly, Pippen's favorite game. Pippen always used the car. Rich always got the boot.

While Rich and Pippen grew closer, Rich became riddled with suspicion about the behaviors of every other family member. Each time he heard the bedroom doorknob twist, a brief terror would overcome him. *This is it*, he would think. But each time it was nothing but Candace getting herself ready to go out or Sarah borrowing a hairdryer or Colton inviting him to go to the movies. Life had become better in all respects excluding the anxiety stemming from the belief, or rather the knowledge, that his family was plotting to kill him. He wished that he was strong enough to let them, to lay out his exposed wrist, to drink from the poison vial, or to do the deed himself with a shotgun, but he could not. Richard wanted things to be better for his family, but Richard did not want to die.

***

On the day before the story was covered on KVTR St. Louis's nightly news and several other local and national news outlets, Richard's wife Candace painted the kitchen cabinets and the fireplace mantle white. It was not a half-white or an eggshell hue, but rather a true white like the center of a lightning bolt. Before the painting started, which was to be done with a compressed air sprayer, Colton and his wife Rachel had covered every inch of the kitchen besides the cabinets with thin plastic sheets and torn trash bags, all adhered with blue painter's tape. Colton had already done his mother the favor of removing all the cabinet doors and placing them on a tarp in the backyard as well as deglossing and priming them.

The cabinets in the old house, the house on Highway G, had been white and so had the fireplace mantle. The rooms there glowed with natural light provided by so many windows. All the house's colors and accent colors—the whites, the creams, the greens, the yellows—were bright and inviting. People had gathered at the old house often. Tables, couches, window seats, counters, and floors were stuffed with people eating food that

Candace had made. Cousins, friends of cousins, aunts, uncles, grandparents, great-grandparents, and if you were lucky your own best friends were guests to large Sunday dinners. Some ended normally and others ended without a fight or argument of some kind between one person or another. But regardless of how they ended, everyone always was happy to be together and under the roof of the house on Highway G.

Gatherings like this were immensely rare at the new house. All the cousins were grown up, all the uncles were divorced and spending time with their new families, and all the money that funded the big dinners was gone. A gloominess rested on the new house, seeping out like fog from Rich and Candace's bedroom. People would gather there occasionally. Candace's parents or her sister, Colton's family, but that was the most you would find. If the old Sunday dinners were a waterfall, these new ones were a leaky faucet.

This reality, this dichotomy of the two houses, angered Sarah. She was only a small child at those bygone grand dinners. She hardly remembered them. When she heard Colton tell stories like the time cousin Luke punched Uncle Jim in the face on Thanksgiving when the missionaries from church were there or the time Colton walked in on their cousin Eric watching porn on the toilet, she would feel cheated out of the true Moore family experience.

She was born far too late, she felt, and most of her life was spent suffering through her mom's sadness and her dad's awful health while her brother was an adult with his own life. He got to go to work and come home to his own house free of the eternal oppression and misery that permeated the place she was asked to call home. But she did not call it home. She made a careful effort to only refer to it as "the house." Sarah was not at "the house" the day before the news would break. She was at a church retreat in Farmington.

***

Candace opened all the windows in the living space that spanned the kitchen, living room, and dining room of the new house. Then she put on her respirator mask and began to paint. The white paint appeared grey as its first sprayed coat landed on the dark cabinets. When Candace finished the first coat, she found that she did not mind the grey color of the cabinets. She took a picture of them with her phone and was about to send it to Sarah. But Candace wanted white cabinets. She needed white cabinets.

After three coats, the stark white of the kitchen cabinets filled the living space with bright reflected natural light. Candace thought of the kitchen on Highway G. She cried.

Colton and Rachel arrived to help install the new gold-colored knobs onto the cabinet doors. Candace had originally wanted silver-colored knobs like the ones they had at the house on Highway G, but Colton and Rachel convinced her to try something new. The result was stunning. Candace touched the knobs over and over, walked around the kitchen and looked at them from various vantage points, and said over and over again how she loved them. It was late now, and the three of them decided to leave the removal of the taped plastic bags and sheets for the next day.

***

That next morning, a Saturday, Rich awoke to see Candace looming over him. She held out a towel draped over both of her arms.

"Candace?" Rich heard himself say.

"Rich, you need to get up," Candace said softly, her eyes red and her face sickly pale.

Rich held his breath as he surveyed the bedroom. Nothing looked out of place. Light came in through the translucent grey curtains that hung over the two windows. He could see the grass, morning sunlight shining brilliantly off each dewy blade. He exhaled, peeled the blankets from himself, and rose from the bed. Candace took a step back as Rich arose. Once standing, Rich observed that a bloody chef's knife rested on the towel that Candace held. She raised her arms toward Rich, and gestured with her head for her husband to pick up the knife.

"Where is Pippen?" Rich tried to look out of the bedroom.

Candace did not answer at first. She simply wept as her hands trembled beneath the towel. After a deep breath, she managed to say, "He's at a friend's house." Then her eyes snapped shut like a vise, revealing weaved wrinkles of age and grief. She turned her head away from Rich. "Please. Take it, Rich. Please."

So this is it. Richard's hands felt bigger, more alive, teeming with blood. Rich watched the fingers wrap around the knife's handle. It was as if someone else, someone who knew how this all was going to end was within Richard, operating levers, forcing Rich to play his part in the unfolding scene.

Rich lifted the knife. Candace looked toward the bedroom door. Richard walked slowly toward it, gripping the knife tightly. Everything was chemical now, a balanced equation of fluids in his brain that triggered all this, that made him complicit.

When he entered the living room, he saw Rachel sitting on the sofa. There were tears in her eyes. She managed only to look at Rich briefly before shifting her gaze to her lap. In a dream-like trance, Richard continued to walk slowly forward. As he came upon the threshold of the kitchen area, he saw Colton. His only son stood with a kitchen knife in his right hand, his other hand clutching a bleeding wound on his right arm. Colton was uneasy, but there were no tears in his eyes.

Richard entered the kitchen. Only once he entered did he take notice of the cabinets. *They are so white*, he thought. *Whiter than the cabinets at the old house, maybe.* He tried to remember exactly how the cabinets in the house on Highway G had looked, but he could not.

"I love you, Dad." Colton could barely say the words. A mixture of fear and shame seemed to stifle his speech.

Rich approached Colton. The blood was gone from Colton's face. Some of it pooled on the taped plastic sheets beneath him.

"Is this how it is going to happen?" Rich heard himself ask.

Colton nodded. "You went crazy, Dad. You were swinging that knife around and you sliced my arm open." Colton struggled to talk. "You rushed toward Mom with the knife—"

A whimper that sounded like Candace's came from the living room.

"—And I had to stop you. It happened so fast, but I did what I needed to do to save Mom and to save this family." Loud shaky breaths escaped Colton's nostrils and generated an unnerving whistling effect each time he exhaled.

Rich closed his eyes and waited. Seconds later, he heard clumsy footsteps rushing toward him. When Rich opened his eyes, one hand was throwing Colton's head into the countertop and the other was thrusting the chef's knife into his son's side. Colton dropped his knife and fell to the ground in a crumpled heap.

Rich dropped the chef's knife and began to walk toward the front door. He pounded his own head with both fists over and over as he walked. Both Rachel and Candace had not witnessed what transpired in the kitchen. They could not bear to. When Rich emerged from the kitchen, the two of them scrambled across the house to find Colton prostrate in a red puddle. They heard the front door open and close.

Candance and Rachel said Colton's name over and over again to the body on the floor. Rachel checked for a pulse. After a few moments, she looked back up at Candace. Rachel could not speak. She just shook her head and sobbed.

The two were jolted out of the moment by the sound of Rich's truck starting out front. They ran outside to find Rich behind the wheel of his truck and backing out of the driveway.

***

As he drove, Rich slammed his head over and over again into his steering wheel.

"You coward!" he yelled. "You goddamned coward!"

He wished he could have let Colton end it all. How nice that would have been for everyone, even for Rich. But there was some force within him. Some power thrust from dormancy. Some pulsating energy in his blood, brains, organs, and bones that would not let him surrender his own life.

In the early days after the stroke, after he had run the company out of business, Richard thought about killing himself. At the time, he told himself that he could not do it because it was morally wrong. Every Christian knew that it was a sin to take one's own life, one of the most abominable before God. But as he looked back now, he knew it was fear that stayed his hand. Fear that came from some unseen place deep within, the same fear that kept the cavemen on edge at night when forest sounds echoed through the wilderness. Rich would extinguish this fear if he was capable, and thought that he might be able to if his mind was fully intact. But the strokes had robbed him of his capacity to fight impulses. He existed in a realm of minute impulses that functioned to keep him alive and nothing beyond that.

Rich drove for six miles before he realized that he was en route to the old house on Highway G. *Yes*, he remembered, *the old kitchen cabinets*. Once more, Richard tried to recall their color. He was almost positive that they were white, but how white he could not say. He thought and thought and thought but the hue of the old cabinets eluded him.

As he turned onto Highway G, he noticed Candace in the car behind him. He wondered what she was doing back there. *Perhaps she too wished to see the old cabinets*, Rich thought. His mind showed him fresh white paint on the kitchen cabinets of the new house. Beneath the cabinets rested a crimson-soaked figure. *What a strange thing for my mind to show me*, Richard thought.

Once past the initial stretch of houses, Highway G was relatively remote. It had not been uncommon for the Moores to drive the whole length of it to their home without passing another vehicle. Richard accelerated. He felt that if he did not reach the old house soon enough that the cabinets would disappear, the whole house even.

Richard heard an engine rev grotesquely. He winced and looked to the sound. Candace drove parallel to him in the other lane. Candace rolled down the passenger window. She leaned over and yelled something at Rich, but he could not hear it. He rolled down his window. Candace continued to yell.

Richard's mind told him that Candace yelled this: "Hurry up! The cabinets are going to disappear!"

What Candace really yelled was this: "Stop the car, Richard! Stop the car!"

Richard yelled, "Okay, sweetie!" Then he accelerated to 95 miles per hour.

They descended onto a long and unoccupied straightaway. The old house was only a few minutes away. The two cars rumbled side by side down the long stretch of road. Candace's nearly inaudible screaming continued. Her eyes, like her screams, were aimed at Rich. She did not see the culvert ahead. Nor did Candace see her wheels drifting off the road.

In the space of an eternal second, Rich watched in his rearview mirror as a car behind him flipped back over front through the air until it made contact with a tall pin oak. After impact, the vehicle teetered briefly before falling right side up, the doors, roof, and windows a twisted broken mess. Richard thought briefly about stopping and helping whoever it was that had crashed. But he could not afford to waste time.

"Hurry up! The cabinets are going to disappear."

Richard heard sirens in the distance. He accelerated.

***

Besides the trees and bushes in the front yard being larger than he remembered, the exterior of the old house looked about as it had when the Moores moved out. Strange cars filled the driveway. Rich wondered who was visiting their home. His parking spot was unoccupied. Like he had thousands of times before, Rich parked his truck. The cradle of familiar pavement grooves welcomed the wheels.

He walked casually to the front door. He would pretend he was a visitor. Little Colton would get a kick out of that. What a fun little trick and a nice little memory it would be.

Rich climbed the two steps of the front porch. The sirens were close now, probably just beyond the hill. *I wonder if there was an accident,* Richard thought. He knocked on the door and then laughed to himself. *Why am I knocking on the door of my own house?* Richard had forgotten about his intended joke. He reached down and pressed his thumb on the opening mechanism of the handle. It was unlocked. Rich opened the door. He walked through the foyer and into the living room. He turned to face the kitchen.

The walls were painted a dark burgundy that made him think of the bathrooms in cheap Italian restaurants. The cabinets were arranged differently and on walls where they had not been before. They were different cabinets entirely. Ornate paisley woodwork covered each darkly stained cabinet door. Rich found it gaudy. Though a cloudless sky scattered solar radiance on the world without, the kitchen seemed as dark as a cellar.

"Where are the cabinets?" Rich asked the walls.

A shotgun pumped behind him.

"Hands up. Now." It was a man's voice. The voice was soft yet firm.

"Why did you get rid of the cabinets?" Rich asked. His hands remained at his side. He was crying now.

"Hands up." The voice spoke louder now to be heard over the wail of the sirens in the driveway.

"They used to be so bright," Richard said, and he fell to the ground.

***

Nothing so tragic, so feverishly twisted had ever occurred in the small town of Franklin, Missouri. At least that was what reporters read from their prompters. The reports varied slightly, but they all shared certain soundbites: "unstable adult male… killed his son… wife in critical condition… youngest daughter with relatives now," and so on.

Rich watched the story from his hospital bed. The people in the report looked familiar. Then the nurse turned it off.

A lot of time passed. Rich did not keep track. He was unaware of the concept of keeping track. People watched him closely and kept his hands secured to his hospital bed. They fed him and said things to him. The things they said sounded like words that Rich thought he knew, but Rich did not seem to know them. Richard made sounds that he thought sounded like words. The people did not seem to understand the words Richard spoke.

More and more time passed. Meals. Questions. Sleep. Television. Repeat. The process felt familiar, a remnant of some past life that he could not remember. Eventually, the questions stopped and his wrists were loosed.

Richard kept eating, kept sleeping, kept looking at a screen. He was moved to a care facility, but he did not perceive it as being different from the hospital. Time lost shape. Minutes passed in years and years passed in seconds.

***

A young man walked into Rich's room. The young man was tall and handsome. He sat next to Rich's bed. The young man reached into his pocket. He produced a shiny little metal boot. The tiny boot made a clink as he set it on the bedside table.

Something reorganized itself in Rich's mind. Sounds and mouth shapes and tongue movements were exhumed from somewhere deep within Rich. He wet his lips and began to cry.

"Pip–Pip–Pippen?"

"Yes, Pop-Pop?" The young man reached out to hold Richard's hand.

"Pippen?" Richard spoke to the walls.

"I'm right here, Pop-Pop." The young man's expression rested at the crossroads of fear and sadness.

"Home?" Richard asked the walls.

"I love you, Pop-Pop." The young man sobbed.

Richard's eyes lowered and his body sunk once more into the medical bed. "Tried…home…"

The boy pushed snot away from his nose with a fist. "Did my dad try to kill you? Did they try to kill you? I heard them talking back then. I know about their plan. My mom doesn't know that I know. She doesn't know that I'm here."

Once more Richard received a brief spark of something lost, and so Richard wept.

The young man put his hand on Richard's shoulder. "You can tell me, Pop-Pop. It's just us."

"I–I–I…" Richard paused for almost ten seconds with his mouth wide open like he was waiting to be spoon-fed. "—want…home."

The young man reached out to wipe a tear as it traveled down Richard's cheek. When the young, unblemished finger touched the salty liquid and the skin it clung to, Richard's head turned like it was spring-loaded, like the switch on some hideous hunting trap.

"No! No! No!" Richard clutched the young man's wrist and shrieked. "No! No! Today! Today now! No tomorrow! No! No! You! Are! Dead! No! No!" He lunged at the young man's throat and toppled from the bed and onto the young man.

There was a long struggle.

And then there wasn't.

NOT HER OWN

"Go back! Go back! We forgot Lemur! I want Lemur! You have to go back!"

"We're already late for the party, Wally. Lemur will be waiting at home. We can't turn around—"

Alaina Lawrence felt the object traveling through the air before it hit her head. There is a certain type of silence that falls before your angry child throws something at you, a silence that generates anger and irritation before the thrown thing makes contact. So while it would be wrong to say that Alaina was surprised when a child's size 11 sneaker pegged her skull, it would not be wrong to say that her simmering fury was brought instantly to a boil.

"Absolutely not! We *do not* ever throw things at people. Especially when they are driving." The screams grew louder. "That could cause an accident. We could crash and die! Is that what you want?"

"I–I–I–I–" Wally labored to catch his breath and stifle his cries. "I just want Lemur to be at the party. He likes parties. He told me he likes parties."

"Well, Lemur told me that you need to be nicer to your mommy. So let's start there. Now no more whining or screaming for the rest of the way to the party, or we won't go!"

"Lemur didn't say that."

"Quiet! Or no birthday party!"

***

The rest of the ride was silent except for the pitter-patter of the rain and the squeaking of the wipers. Wally did give Alaina a good whack on the nose when she was unbuckling his car seat, and Alaina did holler at him some more, and another mom did give a side glance as she walked by with her well-behaved and neatly dressed little girl.

Why did people always see her at her worst? Why couldn't they see how patient and kind she'd been all day during the dozens of tantrums Wally had thrown? *Cosmically appointed parental guilt*, Alaina thought as she set Wally on the ground or rather into a puddle that she had not seen.

"My feet are wet! I want different shoes!"

"I'm sorry, sweetie. I didn't see th—"

This time it was a surprise. A hard fist to the gut.

"No hitting! Ever!"

And with that they walked through the drizzle, one fuming and one screaming, into Mama's Pizza Palace.

***

It seemed like every birthday was here. Alaina had brought Wally to at least three different parties at Mama's Pizza in the last few months. They all followed the same structure. First, there was the small talk with other parents while the kids ate pizza. Then there were the arcade games and claw machines, which Wally whined about not winning. Then there was a cake which was usually bought from a grocery store bakery and was rarely worth the calories. Then came presents. Then everybody went home and napped. That was Alaina's favorite part.

The party was currently at the birthday cake phase. Wally was neck-deep in icing and on his best behavior of the day. Alaina got up from her seat and looked out a large picture window. The rain had picked up and the river that rested some fifty yards from the window frothed with white crashing rapids.

Then she saw her. The old woman. The old woman that had been at every single Mama's Pizza Palace birthday party Alaina had ever brought Wally to. The woman was watching the party fondly. She seemed to savor every little word and every little action from the children. Her eyes were careworn and her wrinkles drew lines that told the story of a life full of emotions expressed or at least well-worn. Alaina had asked other parents, but nobody ever knew who the woman was or what brought her to the restaurant.

Alaina glanced back at Wally. His cake would keep him busy for a while. She went to the woman's table.

"Hi. My name is Alaina Lawrence. You know, I've seen you here at every party I've been to."

"Shhh." The old woman pushed Alaina aside. "I'll miss the best part." The woman widened her eyes. She smiled. Then she shed a few tears and dabbed them neatly with a handkerchief that she produced from her blazer.

Alaina had turned to look for whatever it was the woman saw but noticed nothing of interest.

"My name is Jean Carson, Alaina. Take a seat."

Alaina looked back at Wally.

"Your boy will be fine." She squinted and looked at Wally. "I'll keep an eye on him." The woman had a voice that sounded like it corrected split infinitives and a tone that carried all the authority of Mary Poppins.

Alaina sat down facing Jean Carson and the window which now silhouetted the old woman in mossy storm clouds and gray rain.

"Would you believe that you are the first person who has ever spoken to me here?" Jean's eyes assessed Alaina.

"Well, I just—" here Alaina was about to say *thought you looked lonely* but decided against it. "I like to meet new people, and you look like a woman with a lot of stories."

"What makes you think I have stories?" Jean narrowed her eyes to wrinkly little slits.

"Well, you are at every single party and never as a guest. Something brings you here, and I thought that you would like someone to talk to."

"Something *does* bring me here." Jean paused and looked off at the children. Then she picked up her fork and tapped her plate twice. "The salad."

Alaina looked at Jean's plate. On it was a salad bar creation that looked pale and unappetizing. It looked untouched.

"And you are incorrect. I do not come to every party. I come to one. Just one."

"I know that I've seen you here before."

"I'm not here, Alaina." Jean twirled the air with her pointer finger.

Alaina looked back. Wally was eating a second piece of cake that some other adult must have given him.

"Can I tell you a secret, Alaina. That's why you spoke to me, right? To get my secret. I'll give it to you." Jean brought her chair closer to Alaina's. "This place," she spoke in a whisper now, "is a gateway to the past."

The decor was outdated, it was true. Alaina remembered coming to birthday parties here when she was a girl. She often thought about the kids she came here with and wondered where they were now and whether they were happy.

Jean seemed to read her thoughts. "No, I mean literally, sweetheart. This place can take you back in time."

"Okay. Well, I've always wanted to see a real flapper. Can it take me back to the 20s?"

Jean scoffed. "No. It takes you one place and one place only. Would you like to go there? Or rather would you like to join me there?"

Alaina turned back once more to see Wally.

"Your boy will be fine. Now, go to the salad bar and make yourself a salad with these ingredients and in this order: iceberg lettuce, celery, cucumbers, radishes, and ranch dressing."

"That sounds disgusting. And nobody gets the salad here. It's awful."

"It is awful. That's why I never eat it, but you must make the salad if you want to see what I see."

"And what will happen when I make the salad?"

"You don't believe me. I don't blame you. Just go fix yourself the salad and then we will talk some more."

Alaina walked past the party. It was present time. The children were all in suspense as they watched the birthday girl uncover everything that the colorful paper concealed.

The salad bar was dim, and the restaurant lights cast shadows across all the toppings. Alaina picked up a plate. One by one she added the ingredients just as Jean had instructed. Nothing changed. Although the radio was playing a new song that it hadn't been playing before. She was pretty sure it was the Beatles. Alaina shrugged and finished adding the toppings. There was a waft of cigarette smoke that lingered. *Is someone smoking in here?* Alaina turned around to see a man carrying a fresh pizza to the party with a lit cigarette hanging from his lips.

"You can't smoke in here. This is a children's birthday party."

The man blew a cloud of smoke in Alaina's face. "What's amatter, honey? Little Timmy doesn't like Pall Mall's?" He gave her a wink and walked off, leaving a perfume of pizza grease and nicotine in his wake.

Alaina watched the man disappear around the corner. That was all she felt she could do.

The song on the radio ended. "That was a fresh track from those boys out of Liverpool, the Beatles singing 'Please, Please, Me.' Up next we've got Chubby Checker..."

Then she saw the sign. Having seen it in so many films and photographs, she would have thought that seeing the sign in real life would have been less jarring. This was not the case. Her stomach dropped out and the air grew heavy and acidic. There it rested, screwed four times over into the wall beside the front counter:

WE CATER TO WHITE PEOPLE

Alaina looked down at her salad. *What on earth is*—she felt something touch her shoulder. A hand was there. The skin was smooth and the fingers were delicate and perfectly manicured with glossy red nails.

"I told you to come back to the table after you got your salad, sweetheart."

The woman with the glossy red nails sounded like Jean in tone, but the voice was different now, sleek and dense with sultry heavy breaths. She was gorgeous with her twisted smile and playful wink. She looked angelic and sinister all at once, like the two were constantly competing, going back and forth in their control of this young Jean's essence.

Alaina dropped her salad. The ingredients scattered and the buffet plate rattled on the floor in increasingly rapid wobbles until coming to a complete stop.

"Jeffrey!" Jean called.

The man with the cigarette whipped back around the corner.

"Please clean up this mess for my dear friend, Alaina." She placed a hand once more on Alaina's shoulder.

"Right away, Mrs. Carson." And like that, he was on his knees scooping the ingredients back onto the plate.

"You own this place? You're 'Mama?'"

"I do now, or I did rather. Now come back to the table. It's about to happen."

When they returned to the party room, Alaina looked frantically for Wally.

"He's not here, but you can see him if you squint. He's right—" Jean narrowed her eyes, "—there." She pointed her perfect finger.

Alaina squinted and looked. In a frosted glass sort of layer that overlapped her vision, she saw faintly the figure of her son on what may have been his third piece of cake.

"See? He's just fine. Now take a seat."

Alaina took a deep breath and sat down. The picture window now revealed a brilliant day. A beautiful garden rainbowed in petals rested between the restaurant and the river which crawled lazily across the window. "You said something was going to happen. What is going to happen? Are you going to kill me or eat my soul or something?"

Jean laughed demurely with sealed lips. "No, sweetheart. Just watch. I want your feedback." Jean patted Alaina's hand and smiled at her. "Oh, here they are right now. Come on." Jean stood up and pulled Alaina along with her.

Across the restaurant, a man came through the door holding a little girl's hand. She was dressed in a little jumper dress with purple flowers. As soon as they stepped in, her father came to an abrupt stop. His eyes were on the sign drilled into the wall next to the front counter. Slowly, carefully he turned around to leave. The little girl did not turn. She had seen the party and her friend, the birthday girl who was beckoning her to come eat pizza.

Jean walked in swift wide strides to the door. "Mr. Franklin, please stay. I know my daughter, Charity, loves your daughter so much."

Mr. Franklin said nothing. He looked from the sign to Jean.

"Oh, please ignore that. You are welcome here." Jean reached down to the little girl's other hand. "Come on, Ruby. I've got some pizza all ready just for you."

Mr. Franklin held firm, but his daughter was already halfway to the party hand in hand with Jean. After a moment, he walked cautiously to the party room, slowing his pace every few steps and looking over his shoulder.

Alaina walked back to the party as well. After chatting briefly with Mr. Franklin, Jean came back and joined Alaina at their table.

"So how was I? Wasn't I kind? Don't they feel welcome? Shouldn't they?" Jean's feigned glee felt stale to Alaina.

Alaina looked once more at Mr. Franklin. His hands were in his pockets and he had retreated from the party to a corner.

"I mean what am I supposed to do differently? I didn't make all this happen. I inherited this prejudice, this reality. But I am better now. That was good, wasn't it? Tell me it was good."

Alaina said nothing. She was squinting a look at Wally. He was finished with cake and was watching lazily, hand pushed into his cheek, as the birthday girl opened more presents.

Jean shrieked, pulling Alaina back to the past. Her daughter's party guests took no notice. Jean seemed to have some control over this reality, of what they perceived. "I can't stop it. No matter how nice I am to that man. I've lived this day thousands of times. I've given him money. I've apologized. I've made it the best damn day of his daughter's life, and still nothing changes. You see that little girl?" Jean pointed at Mr. Franklin's daughter.

Alaina nodded.

"She is the reason my daughter died in college." Jean sniffled and wiped snot daintily from her nose. "The original day of this party, I did nothing. That's not true. I actually asked them to leave before Mr. Franklin turned around himself. And my daughter, my Charity, was furious. She didn't understand why they had to leave. She later would tell me that it was that moment that lit a fire in her, that made her want to march and protest, that got her shot by those stupid soldiers at Umpqua State University. So day after day I come here. I get my salad. And I am kind. I am so generous and so kind, but it changes nothing. Every time I go back, Charity is still dead."

"Have you tried taking down the sign?"

"You don't think I've thought of that? No. You don't understand. Your generation never does. If I take that down, this restaurant will go under. There are hardly any black people in this town. But there are plenty of white people that won't go to a restaurant that serves black people."

"But what if it saves your daughter?"

"It wouldn't. It would just embolden her. She'd probably die sooner. It's not fair. I shouldn't have to suffer like this. I've made it right. I've fixed it. Oh God, I love my little girl so much. I just want her back." Jean put her face in her palms. "God please," she screamed, "Give me back my daughter!"

Alaina reached out to her. "Jean—"

"Be kind to your child. Love him. Love him so he is safe. Love him so you can have him. *Having* the child. That's the thing. You've got to *have* them. Because when you don't. When you don't…" Jean looked out the window at the river. Then she took a bite of pizza and disappeared.

Alaina looked around the restaurant. It was empty and the lights were out. "Wally?" She looked down at the table and saw Jean's pizza slice. She took a bite.

All at once she was at the party, the party where Wally was now dismantling balloon decorations and kicking them all over the floor. She looked around for Jean but could not find her.

"Time to go, sweetie," Alaina called across the room.

Wally was rundown. It was an hour and a half past nap time. "Okay, Mommy."

***

Wally fell asleep on the drive home. Alaina carried him carefully to his bed and tucked him in with Lemur. Then she gently pulled his wet shoes and socks off and put them by the heater to dry. She watched him for a while as he slept. Just as

Wally let out a little yawn, her pocket started to buzz. She pulled out her phone. It was a local number. Alaina closed Wally's door.

"Hello."

"Hello, is this Alaina Lawrence?"

"Yes, may I ask who this is?"

"Oh my God. I finally found you." The voice on the other end grew shaky. "My name is Charity Bell. My mother, Jean Carson, died when I was a little girl. She took her own life on my ninth birthday. I know it's strange to get a call like this, but I found this journal of my mother's and she mentions you as someone she really admired. I'd love to meet you and get to know my mother a little better by talking to you. Would that be okay?"

Alaina opened Wally's door and watched as he rolled over and pulled his blanket up. Then she closed it once more. "Yes, I would enjoy that. Your mother was an incredible woman."

OURO DE TOLO

I hate things like this. People think that I hate parties altogether or that I'm not sociable. Not true. When I am with my close friends, my real friends, my friends that don't work for Vission Corp, I dance and sing and wisecrack and bust chops and do impersonations of Donald Trump or Mr. Burns or Bale's Batman. But here I stand in a corner next to the refreshments table, silent and observant like Hercule Poirot. My eyes glide over all the corporate glad-handers.

Most of them are actually great people on their own. Laura over by the impressionist ocean painting always remembers everyone's birthday and sends a little private gift to them in their mailbox, and she always has gum that she shares, the nice kind that pops out of the bubbles like over-the-counter meds. But in here she's laughing too loud at stories and she's exaggerating or fabricating stories of her own. They all do. Show and tell from hell.

I think about the only show and tell I remember from my childhood. The second-grade teacher Mrs. Hermann called me to the front to share. I panicked. I'd forgotten to bring in something. As I stood up, the little hot wheel bus in my pocket shifted slightly. So I pulled it out and told the class about how I'd gotten the toy bus. It was at the place where I'd received private surfing lessons in Hawaii last summer. I told them about Rico, the instructor who said I was the best student he ever had. I told them about the massive tsunami wave that I'd rode alongside Rico. I told them about how we high-fived at the end and how he promised to come visit us on the mainland someday.

A week later my mom and dad came home from parent-teacher conferences. They asked when I'd gone to Hawaii without them and why they weren't invited. As a punishment, I was grounded from video games for two weeks. My dad also pulled me close and said this:

"When you lie and make up a fake life and pass it as truth, you are saying that your *real* life—all of this—," he gestured to the four-bedroom house we shared with my grandma, "is not good and not worth talking about. You have a good life. Don't insult God and his graciousness."

As I imagine my Dad's voice and how it sounded when he reprimanded me, a man at the party approaches my corner. I recognize him, although we've never shared a word. He's not a storyteller. He's not a corporate party jock. He's an observer like me. Ethan or Evan, I think. And based on the few emails I've seen with him in the CC, he's pretty high up in Vission Corp's

Product Management division. His eyes are weary, and he walks with an awkward confidence like he's thrown back a few.

"Hi," he says.

"Hi."

"You—" He points to me with the hand that's holding his drink. "You are like—" he shifts the drink hand pointer finger to himself. "Me."

I smile and try to keep it light. This guy could probably get me fired if he wanted. "Really? How's that?" I ask.

"You think this is all bull shit, don't you? Don't you?" His eyes are wide and he's gripping my shoulder now.

"This party?"

"Yes. This party. This company. This culture. This century. This overpriced scotch in my glass. All of it. All of the windbags out there telling stories and anecdotes, each wilder than the last, everyone outdoing everyone for a gasp or a smile or a laugh. It's. All. Shit. Right?"

I exhale. "Yes. I hate it. It's exhausting to me, and I don't even participate. How can they just make up so much crap?"

"What did you say?" Ethan or Evan's eyes narrow.

"Well, I mean how can they just make this stuff up and tell it all with a straight face? What kind of person does that?" I am defensive for some reason that I don't yet know.

Ethan or Evan laughs. He sets his drink down on the refreshments table and laughs some more. He slaps his knee and eventually goes into a coughing fit. When the coughing subsides, he looks at me all ice and stone. "They don't make any of it up. It's all true. Very true and very real."

Now I laugh. "So Sindra Basi saved three children from a flaming passenger train in Ghana last year? And, and Kevin Yamata was really taken hostage in Columbia? And Marcus Boswell really—"

"Yes." Ethan or Evan pauses. "And no. Tell you what. You got plans tonight?"

I shake my head.

"Do you want to know where all the stories come from?"

"How do you mean?"

"Do you want to know? Yes or no?"

"Well, does it mean we're gonna get out of *here*?" I rebuke the whole party with one tossed glance.

Ethan or Evan nods.

"Then yes."

***

Ethan or Evan's place is in the Village. It's a four-story house with a massive private garage filled with cars whose makes and models I did not even know existed. The interior of the house is white. White walls. White furniture. White floors. White counters. White light. White modern paintings with small geometric black shapes and lines. White curtains. White blinds.

We are seated on a modern white sectional that sits within the floor, the very top of the sectional's frame flush with the floor's black-veined white marble. Ethan or Evan hasn't said a word since we left the party. He reaches into his suit coat and pulls something out. It is a business card. He scoots over to me and puts it right up to my face. It's white and it's blank. He tilts it back slowly and glossy numbers printed in white reflect in the light. It looks like a telephone number.

"Right here." He flicks the card. "This is where all the stories come from." He hands me the card. "Go ahead. Call it."

I get my phone out and dial the number. No ringtone. Just a voice. "Hello, Wesley. What story would you like to tell?"

"What?" I cover the microphone and look to Ethan or Evan. "How do they know my name? What is this?"

Ethan or Evan just smiles.

The voice on the phone speaks again. "I see this is your first time calling. Please have your referrer explain our service to you and then give us a call back if you like." The call ends.

Ethan or Evan stands now by a large floor-to-ceiling window. "Any story you want to tell, you can tell." As he speaks, mechanical blinds recede into the ceiling above. Ethan or Evan surveys the street below. "It comes at quite the premium. But living—*really* living—is the only thing worth spending money on, isn't it?" He slams a clenched fist against the glass and the window thuds softly. "Military-grade insulated glass. I couldn't break it no matter how hard I tried."

I nod and an awkward chuckle escapes my lips.

Ethan or Evan grabs a bottle of Macallan from the bar and hurls it against the window. The bottle shatters and falls to the ground. Streams of golden scotch drip down the window. "See? Unbreakable." He picks up a tufted white accent chair and flings it against the window. The glass is unscathed. "See? Not a fracture. Not a scratch."

"Thank you so much for having me to your beautiful home, but I think I ought to leave." I step up and out of the seating area.

"No. Don't leave. I need to tell *my* story. I've never told anyone, and I feel I can tell you. I *know* I can. I'm sorry. Sit back down. When the story is over, I'll have Oliver take you home. Alright?"

"Alright." I return to the sofa but now on the corner, as far from Ethan or Evan as possible. "What's the story?"

"This is the story." Ethan or Evan closes his eyes and takes a deep breath. "About a year ago, someone at one of those parties told a story that chronicled their journey into the seedy underworld of Thailand to save the kidnapped child of a fruit vendor who'd gotten in deep with the wrong guys. When the story was done, everyone was amazed except for me. I laughed. 'There is no way,' I said or something like that.

"The woman who told the story glared at me. 'I swear to God and on my grandmother. All of that happened, and it happened just like that.' Then she pulled a card from her purse and slid it into my suit coat, the same card I just showed you.

"I called the number. I heard the same thing you heard. After some further discussion with the woman who had given me the card, I discovered that this business provided authentic manufactured experiences for customers. Any situation you wanted to experience with the outcome that you desired. You want to sword fight a child trafficker and live to tell the tale? You want to save passengers on a sinking ship? Anything you want to live, you can. But the trickier the story, the higher the price.

"I asked the person on the phone if the people in the situations were paid actors.

"'If they were paid actors,' she said, 'then these wouldn't be true stories.'

"She explained to me that they were all real people in real situations and that they were paid handsomely for their participation. I thought the whole thing was stupid. That it was such a rotten bourgeois sort of vanity. But curiosity got the better of me. Like a fool, I started to rationalize. What else would I do with all this money? And it was a comfort knowing that these people who participated would be paid well. They were probably down on their luck. I'd be doing them a favor. So I called the number back.

"A week later I was in an office with my story manager. We decided that I would do something simple. There would be a mugging in São Paulo, Brazil, and I would fight off the muggers to save my own life. Simple. Small scale."

Ethan or Evan takes a draft from an unshattered bottle of Macallan that Oliver had set on the coffee table just moments before.

"So I fly down to São Paulo for some business. I had arranged with my story manager to meet with all the participants of the story beforehand. The story manager found this strange, but he made the arrangements all the same.

"I took a taxi to a favela in a district called São Faustino. There I met the man who would lead the group of muggers. He was a tall, thin, muscular man who introduced himself as Marquinhos. He was very friendly and had me come right into his slapdash brick home which was built off of five other little brick homes and roofed by a single sheet of corrugated steel. I had learned a little bit of Portuguese in preparation for the trip and was able to give and respond to the traditional greetings.

"Marquinhos then pulled me close and pointed to the skin on his arm. 'Como diga *negro* em Inglês?' he asked me. I was not sure what he had asked at first, but he repeated the question and the gesture over and over again. When I finally believed that I was understanding him, I was worried to answer as I did not want to offend anyone nor appear ignorant. 'Em Inglês nos dizemos *black* ou *preto*,' I told him in slow timid syllables." Ethan or Evan laughs and wipes tears from his eyes.

"You see *preto* or *black* in Portuguese is like the N-word down there. Marquinhos and his friends got a kick out of this. They marched me around the favela and down to the little market and had me recite my answer to everyone. Everyone laughed and slapped me on the back and called me an 'Americano doidinho.' They were all so kind. Everyone but Marquinhos's wife." Ethan or Evan sets the bottle down and goes back to the window.

"When we got back to Marquinhos's house, his wife was there with the kids. She screamed at me. She spoke very fast. I couldn't make out anything she was saying, but she took off one of her Havaianas and beat me with it until I left the house. All the while, Marquinhos apologized to me. Right before I walked through the front door, I made out the word *husband* and the word *kill.* I stopped in my tracks.

"I told her as best I could that I was not going to kill anyone, that this was a good thing, that I would make sure that Marquinhos and all his friends would be paid very well. That it might help them get into a better situation. Then she spit at me and slammed the thin rickety door in my face.

"In the street, Marquinhos reassured me and thanked me so much for this opportunity. He told me I was a good man. That I was sent from God. That I was an answer to prayers. And I believed it.

"Later that night I walked down Avenida São Vicente de Almeda like we planned. I was supposed to be lost. Marquinhos and his friends surrounded me. One of them pulled out a pistol and told me to hand over my money. As rehearsed, I disarmed the guy (the gun was unloaded) and proceeded to struggle and fight against the rest. Then the cops showed up. They arrived quickly because they were in on it too, you see. Except they did something that was outside of my agreement, or at least I thought it was. Always read the full contract!" He screamed at the walls and ceiling. "What the officers did was shoot and kill every single one of those men. I screamed for them to stop, but the barrage of bullets didn't cease until Marquinhos and all his friends were just a pile of bloody flesh."

Ethan or Evan comes close to me. He reaches down to the coffee table and pulls upwards on the surface of it to reveal a large storage compartment. In it, I see a scattered pile of envelopes. They are all addressed to the same person: A Esposa de Marquinhos. They've all been returned to the sender.

"What happened, Wesley, is that the organization that provides stories makes arrangements with the municipalities in which they operate, municipalities that are immensely impoverished and filled with desperate people. The local authorities clean up any loose ends so that the organization remains secret from the general public, the uh 99% as the lawmakers say. Then the families of the story participants are paid very well—a real life-changing injection of wealth."

Ethan or Evan runs his fingers across the envelopes. "I've tried to atone, but I can't. I never will. That's my story. Oliver will take you home now."

"Couldn't you expose the company?" I say. "Bring them down? This all has to be illegal. Wouldn't that atone?"

He laughs at this. "I am complicit in their crime. With the information they have on me and access I gave them to my personal life, they would have me undone before I could even do so much as point a finger in their direction."

"But if you truly want to make it right then you would try anyway."

Ethan or Evan smiles. "I like you, Wesley. I hope you mean that. Because they'll be coming for you after tomorrow."

"A complimentary Uber is waiting outside, Wesley," says a voice from behind me. I turn to see Oliver. "And your plane takes off in two hours, sir. We should leave immediately."

I open my mouth to speak, but Ethan or Evan is already disappearing down the hallway.

***

The next week at Vission Corp, I don't see Ethan or Evan anywhere.

On Thursday a police detective shows up at the office. She asks to speak to several employees, including myself.

When it's my turn to be questioned, the detective leads me to a small office that I've never seen before. The walls of the office are covered with hundreds of paper cranes, each one made with green American bills. The office has a tall wooden stool in the center where I am asked to sit.

"What office is this?" I ask.

"I dunno. This is where they told me I could interview people," the detective says.

There are no windows. No breeze. But I swear I can see the wings of each crane fluttering as though they were trying to go somewhere. Somewhere bright and sunny where they could be enjoyed. I reach out to touch one of them, but I stop when the detective begins her interview.

The detective pulls out her phone and starts an audio recording. "State your full name and address."

"Wesley Neil Porter. 232 Kent Avenue, Apartment 12, Brooklyn."

"Thank you, Mr. Porter. CCTV footage, as well as various testimonies, indicate that Eric Hill spent much of his last night in the US with you."

"Eric Hill?"

The detective rolls her eyes and pulls a picture from a manila folder. It's him. It's Ethan or Evan, or Eric rather.

"That is correct. I was over at his house."

"Were you close to Mr. Hill?"

"No."

The officer looks at me furtively as she continues to circle me slowly. "What did you talk about at Mr. Hill's residence that night?"

"Well. Um. We uh—he—"

The detective's eyes narrow. "'We he' what?"

I say nothing. My eyes are fixed on a little paper crane on the wall to my left. I swear that I see Benjamin Franklin's lips on one of the paper wings.

"Okay, well here's how it looks for you, buddy. You left Mr. Hill's house at 11:23 PM, and two hours later Mr. Hill boarded a private jet to Brazil. About 24 hours after that, Mr. Hill took his own life in a São Paulo slum. As far as we know, you are the last person he spoke to before leaving the country. So I'll ask you one more time before I take you into custody, what did you talk to Mr. Hill about that night?"

"I don't want to tell the story."

"What? Why the hell not?"

"It's—it's not my story to tell."

"And what *is* your story?"

"I don't have one."

"Not yet. But I am sure you will. Did Mr. Hill mention anything about a white business card?"

"What?" My eyes bolt from the table to the officer.

The officer smiles. "So you know. Okay then." The officer flips her little notepad shut. "You are free to go."

"Are you trying to stop them?"

She grins. "I'm just trying to get the story right."

***

My apartment is a small little number. It's a studio. Everything is secondhand Ikea. Everything except the bed. That was a wedding gift and it's the only thing I kept after the divorce.

I toss my keys on the kitchen counter, walk over to the bed, and fall onto it backwards. I stare at the ceiling, and my mind casts paper cranes from that strange office onto the popcorn ceiling. *What was that place?*

I look to my left. There is something in the shadows on my nightstand. Something I don't recognize. My fingers reach out and switch the lamp switch. Sitting atop my nightstand is a paper crane. The pristinely folded bill looks freshly printed. I open it. On the front of the bill is a single word written in permanent marker: "Atonement"

Below where the crane rested is a folded piece of paper. As I unfold the paper, I see a small note written on it.

> *I, Eric Heller Hill, residing at 176 Washington Place, Greenwich Village, NY, declare this to be my Will, and I revoke any and all wills and codicils I previously made. To Wesley Neil Porter of 232 Kent Avenue, Apartment 12, Brooklyn, NY, I leave everything.*
>
> *December 9th, 2023*

I look back to the fifty-dollar bill. I flip it to the backside. There is one more message: "They'll be coming for you. Hope this helps."

ALL-AMERICAN SHOOTING STAR

Jimmy Cane was on his way to confess something. The need to confess had festered and frothed for years. Lately, it brought such mental and emotional anguish that Jimmy had started to see and hear things. Strange things. Familiar to him but long gone. Nearly forgotten things. He hoped his confession would banish the visions and the voice. If it did not, Jimmy feared what he might do.

The last confession Jimmy could remember was to his youth pastor when he was thirteen years old. Jimmy had confessed that he looked at porn. He expected the pastor to open the worn King James that rested on his desk and remind Jimmy of the flames and brimstone that awaited carnal minds who bent to impulse. But the skinny bearded middle-aged pastor with a widow's peak just smiled and told Jimmy that even though watching porn was wrong, it was still a sin that could be repented of. He told young Jimmy that confessing was the hardest part, that he was a great young man, and that he was very proud of

Jimmy and knew that God was too. Somehow Jimmy had left that meeting with a higher opinion of himself: a shocking feat for a boy who, only moments before, was sure his ticket to hell was all but stamped.

That was a long time ago. Before he was a national hero. Before he received the Presidential Medal of Freedom. Before he received a full-ride citizenship scholarship to Northwestern. Before he was a state representative. Before he was a senator in Washington. Jimmy Cane was, in fact, a senator as he walked down the hall that morning. He was not sure he would be a senator at the day's end.

The path to Senate majority leader Frank Love's office had never felt so long, and the record-breaking summer heat made the walk feel longer still. The air conditioning in the Capitol Building was out, leaving the whole place damp and hot like a baker's oven. With each step toward his confession, Jimmy sweated more and more. He could feel the little beads hitting the collar of his starched white shirt. But the shirt wasn't so white now. It was a grey wet mess. Jimmy tore off his suit coat and tossed on the floor. "I won't need it anymore anyway," he thought.

A random staffer to some other senator picked the thing up. "Senator Cane? You dropped your coat."

Jimmy Cane did not hear this. He heard only his own heavy breathing and a voice that had arrived in his head a few strides back.

They are in for a shock. Oh, yes they are. Let's shock 'em, Jimmy. Let's blow the roof off this place.

A stairwell. The steps loomed like the tongue of some terrible geometric demon. The tongue moved and the stairs spoke.

C'mon, Jimmy. This whole thing is shit. You know that. You've always known it. Let's tear it down.

"Stop it," Jimmy said to the stairs.

"I'm sorry, sir." The staffer's face flushed. "I'll just hold on to it then."

Fuck them all, Jimmy. Fuckin' let's do it. You've wanted to for so long. I know it. You act like you don't, but I know better, buddy.

"Stop it." Jimmy yelled now.

The staffer ran off, leaving the coat behind on the polished floor.

The stairs were once more stairs.

***

A dizzy spell hit Jimmy as he reached the top of the staircase. His vision began to darken. "Am I going to make it?" Jimmy thought. He clutched the banister. He closed his eyes and stood leaning against the handrail. "Don't burn up," Jimmy whispered to himself. "Don't disappear. Everyone has to know. You'll be free then. You have to be free." His eyes opened. A long hallway laid before him, Senator Love's door resting at the farthest end of it. Jimmy released his grip and stood on his own. "I can do this. After everything I've done, this will be the easy part."

***

"That you, Jim?" Senator Love said abstractly, his eyes buried in his computer.

"Yes, sir. May I—"

"Dammit, Jim. Stop calling me 'sir' and stop saying 'may I' all the goddamn time. Stop acting like a junior Senator."

This little cock sucker bosses you around, tells you how to act. You just take it like a little bitch. What happened to you?

Jimmy winced and wiped the perspiration from his forehead. "Of course. I'm sorry." He sat himself down in the armchair that sat opposite Love's desk. The walls of the office were covered in pistols, rifles, muskets, and all other sorts of firearms. Each sat polished and unfired behind a glass shadowbox.

"And no more 'I'm sorry,' alright? You got nothin' to be sorry about." Love smiled, closed his computer, and removed his pair of readers. "Now to what do I owe the honor? What brings our golden boy to the office of this old codger?" Senator Love asked, and he massaged his wrinkled, liver-spot-ridden scalp.

"Well," Jimmy said, and he gulped like a cartoon cat, "about that 'no more saying sorry' business."

Tell 'em, Jimbo. Blow it all up.

"Is this about that ammo limitation bill?" Love kicked his feet up onto his desk. "I'll admit, I am disappointed you couldn't get some dems to cross over. But you seem a little tired lately, so I'll let it slide. But don't let shit happen again, boy. You are our little pied piper. We need you playing that sweet tune of yours, that golden oldie."

He says sing and you sing? Are you a little circus monkey, Jimbo? They give you peanuts?

"It isn't that." Jimmy fiddled with the cuff of his left sleeve. "I have something I have to tell you, to tell a lot of people really. But I want to tell you first so you can help me decide how to tell the public." Jimmy loosened his tie and unbuttoned his shirt's top button. The heat of the room seemed to focus on him, like focused sunlight through a magnifying glass.

Love brought his feet back to the floor and sat up straight in his tufted leather office chair. "And what is it you need to tell me?"

Jimmy Cane looked over his shoulder. "Could I close the door first?"

Senator Love nodded.

Don't close it. Keep it wide open. Yell it through th—

Jimmy closed the door gingerly and returned to his seat. When he got the courage to lift his head, he took a long deep breath. "I'm a fraud," he exhaled.

"Really? And how is that?" Love's eyes narrowed and his usually puckish countenance melted away.

"Well, that story that made me famous, that got me scholarships, that got me elected? It is founded on a lie." Jimmy couldn't stand to make eye contact with Senator Love, so he stared down at his lapel as he adjusted and readjusted his American flag pin. The pin had eyes and a mouth. The pin spoke.

Yes, Jimbo. Tell him who we really are.

Senator Love's grin returned. "Go on then."

"Well, I—I. When I was sixteen years old I took a gun to school. I wanted to shoot people. I wanted to kill people." Aggression gushed from each syllable now. "I wanted to kill lots of people because my life was hell and they all kept kicking me back into the fire each time I tried to climb out. I wanted to make people pay. Sometimes I still want to."

A soft chuckle escaped Senator Love's lips.

What's this fucker laughing about?

"I am serious. I wanted to kill people, and I still do sometimes. I brought a rifle to school that day. You see, I walked into the front entrance ready to unload, but I was too late." Jimmy stared at a framed AR-15-style rifle that sat directly behind and above Senator Love. He remembered what it felt like that morning. To hold it and to wipe someone off of the planet. "Someone else was already shooting up the school. I panicked. I hid myself behind a door, but then the shooter was walking toward me."

"This is wonderful, Jim. So what did the shooter do when he saw you? Did he say, 'this school isn't big enough for the both of us?'" And like that Love's feet were back up on the desk.

This smart ass bastard. We ought to shoot him right in the dick and let him bleed out.

"What? No. This isn't a joke." Jimmy made eye contact with Love for the first time since he'd arrived in the room. "You know what happened. The shooter didn't say anything because I shot him four times in the head."

Pop. Pop. Pop. Pop.

"We all know you are a hero, Jim. No need to recount this old tale." Love opened up his computer once more and reached for his glasses.

"Did you hear what I said? I brought a gun to my school. Everyone thinks I used one of his guns. They think I disarmed him. My entire career, my entire life is all founded on a lie."

Love shook his head. "No. No it is not. There was a shooter. You killed him. You saved many lives. Who cares what you were doing before? Hmm? I sure don't. Now I need you to set up a meeting with Senator—"

What a piece of shit. He used us, Jimbo. He fuckin' used us.

"Yes it *is* a lie. Everyone thinks I was a good guy with a gun. But I wasn't." Jimmy pleaded, his eyes projecting a longing, a longing to be chastised, to be punished.

I'm not scared of shit. You hear me?

"That's not how America sees it. Let's not ruin it for them." As Love typed away at his computer, his features began to tighten and his eye twitched.

"I'm sorry, but I can't go on like this any longer. I'll be calling a press conference tomorrow. I'm going to tell the truth."

"No." Love stood up. "No, you are not."

You gonna let this punk ass cock gobbler boss you around? You a pussy, Jimbo?

Jimmy Cane shot up from his chair, a spark of something different, of fire in his eyes. "Why don't you understand? This is killing me, Frank. If I don't come clean about this, I am going to lose it. I am going to implode. Don't make me. I want to do what's right."

"You talk about 'what's right' like a child," Love snarled. "What's right? How about the gun legislation you've passed? How about the fact that since the 'Good Guy with a Gun' Act passed, not a single innocent child has been killed in a school shooting? And you know why? Because of *you*. Because of you we've got armed guards at every school and a pistol on the hip of most teachers. Because of you parents aren't afraid to drop their kids off at school. And you want to throw that all away?"

I know I do. Burn it all to shit.

"I can't live like this, Frank. If those laws are good, they'll stay. What's it matter if I passed them?"

Like a cobra, Love whipped himself in front of Jimmy's chair and grabbed him by the back of the neck. Jimmy could not believe such a frail old man was capable of such lightning maneuvers. "Listen, you little shit. I knew you brought a gun to school. There was evidence enough of that. Lots of us knew it, but we saw an opportunity. We pulled strings. We made calls. We made a hero. We made schools safer. So don't fuck this all up, okay? Because I shit you not, we can make your life a hell of a lot worse than it is right now. There's a lot of money tied up in all this, and if you go throwing yourself a pity party on national television then a lot of good people are gonna lose their jobs. You don't want to do that, do you?"

Good people? Hmph. Nobody is good. There is no good, Jimbo.

Jimmy lowered his head and receded into himself. He felt something shift. The solar flares that heated the world and heated the room entered his body. Jimmy was a blazing centrifuge. And in that centrifuge, the duality of his mind distilled into something new and whole and bursting with crackling fresh energy.

So that's what it's about. What it's always been about. Wealth and power. The new symbols of Old Glory. Or are they new? Or have these always been America's only gods? All at once, Jimmy's mind brought his whole life into focus, the sleepwalking blur that had been the last 36 years now crisply defined in a mosaic of memories, of choices and of influences that had brought him here. Jimmy Cane, the party's ace in the hole. Run here, Jimmy. Say this, Jimmy. Don't say that, Jimmy. Remember the optics, Jimmy.

Yes. America is burning, and the fire is so big that it obscures reality, so big that we all bought tickets, so big that we enjoy watching, so big that we say, "fire is all there is, all there ever will be, and so I'll burn too." But could we snuff it out? Could we finally see the ashes and the truth that lies in their flakes? Would we want to see it? It doesn't matter what we want. That's all that's mattered so far and look where it got us.

Yes. I can pour the first bucket. No fire wants to be put out, but it doesn't want to burn either. It's just reacting. Everything and everyone is just reacting constantly. And now I am going act, to operate outside the fire, to be the first wave of a deluge that will end America as we know it. Good riddance.

"Now," Love's voice snapped Jimmy from his thought, "get the fuck out of my office." Love's bony claw wrenched onto Jimmy's shoulder. "And never mention any of this again."

"Okay." Jimmy stood up to leave. Just before he walked out, he stopped. "Frank," Jimmy called over his shoulder, "do you ever think about using one of your guns to shoot people?"

"Constantly. That's what they're made for, isn't it?"

***

That morning Jimmy Cane had wanted to confess. A new desire possessed him now. Well, not an entirely new desire.

On his lap sat an AK-47. The weapon, its grey gunmetal twinkling in Jimmy's eyes, had been a gift from Senator Love on the day that Jimmy was sworn into office as a senator. The firearm was illegal for civilians. But thanks to all of Jimmy's hard work on Capitol Hill, all government employees were recognized by law as members of the US military. So the gun and the five clips of nearly one hundred rounds each were perfectly legal for Jimmy Cane to own.

To kill. That was a necessity. A pleasure, but also a necessity. But who? When he was a boy it was obvious who to target. The teachers and the kids who bullied him, who kicked him when he was down. But who carried the blame here? Was it Frank Love? No. No, Frank Love was just a weak little puppet clinging to the power someone else had handed him. And who handed him that power? Of course.

Why hadn't it come to him immediately? Yes, *this was going to feel good,* Jimmy thought. *If they won't let me confess then I'll commit further to my sin. Time to smother it all. The truth shall set us all free, and what better way to tell the truth than to show it?*

Tomorrow, the world will meet the real Jimmy Cane.

They're gonna to hate him.

***

At 9:17 am the next day, Jimmy Cane and his military-grade automatic rifle entered the national headquarters for the American Gun & Weapon Association.

By 10:31 am Jimmy Cane had shot and killed 167 people.

At 10:32 am Jimmy Cane put a bullet through his own head.

At 12:43 pm an official press release from the D.C. Police Department was released. This is what it said:

> **At 9:17 am this morning a gunman, armed with a semi-automatic assault rifle, entered the national headquarters of the American Gun & Weapon Association in Arlington, Virginia. The gunman proceeded to open fire on all occupants of the building that he came across, methodically moving his way up each floor. On the third floor, the gunman was met by retaliatory fire from Senator Jimmy Cane who was in the building for a meeting with AGWA leadership. Senator Cane shot and killed the gunman but was shot himself three times during the exchange. Paramedics declared both the gunman and Senator Cane dead when they arrived at the scene at 10:35. The total number of fatalities is not known, but police and paramedics are working hard to identify bodies and notify families and loved ones.**
>
> **We are thankful for Senator Cane, his bravery, his love of country, and the legacy that he solidified with this selfless act. Our hearts are with the families of the victims. Please**

direct yourself to the AGWA website for information on how to help those affected by this tragedy.

***

In his final moments, Jimmy Cane said these words aloud to himself: "God, I'm sorry I killed all these people. And I'm sorry I didn't do it sooner."

Nobody else heard them.

BANANA CIGARETTE

It was October 17th, 2084 and stupid opinions were illegal in the United States of America. Up until 2059 stupid opinions had been very legal, very common, and extremely monetized. You could make lots of money off stupid opinions back before 2059. Some people made zounds of money talking about how stupid the stupid opinions were. Other people made zounds of money defending stupid opinions and building a platform on the idea that—no matter how stupid an opinion was—it was each American's right to have and promote stupid and dangerous opinions. Few people talked about worthwhile opinions then. Worthwhile opinions were not exciting. They did not get likes or views. If something didn't get likes or views back then, it didn't exist.

But it was 2084. A stupid opinion had not been shared online for 25 years. The internet had atrophied. It was just a big store now. The big store mostly sold banana flavored cigarettes. Almost everyone smoked banana flavored cigarettes.

***

On October 17th, 2084, Buck McKork wheeled himself into the local House of Babes. Anyone who wanted to have their opinion on the internet had to go to a House of Babes to have their words posted by a Pure Child.

The House of Babes waiting area was empty except for the reception desk housing a greasy teenage boy who was drowning in the collar and cuffs of a suit that he must have inherited from a much larger relative. "Name, sir?"

"Buck McKork."

The teenager hastily jotted something on his tablet. Then cleared his throat performatively. "Mr. McCuck—"

"McKork," Buck McKork interrupted.

"Sorry. Mr. Mc*Crack*," the boy chuckled. "You are about to go before House of Babes Tribunal #3425 of Lake County, Missouri. You will tell them your opinion and they will decide whether it is posted to your government issued social media profile. What is your social media ID number?"

McKork gave the number.

"Thank you. Now, Mr. Mc*Crank*," the boy said with a poorly delivered wink. "The Pure Children are a protected group of the United States Government." The spiel was so rehearsed that McKork half expected it to come with a little bag of peanuts. "They have been raised in cultural and moral isolation. The only instruction they have received is in the English Language. They interact only with each other and have no knowledge of any history, popular culture, current events, etc.

You are only allowed to state your opinion. Any context or preambles could disrupt the nature of the Pure Children and thus hamper their ability to assess opinions as outlined in Amendment 29 of the United States Constitution. If you provide any context to your opinion, you will be sentenced to 15 years in prison without trial. Do you agree to these terms?"

"Yep."

The secretary pointed to a screen on the desk and handed McKork a stylus. "Sign here."

McKork scribbled his initials.

"Thank you for coming to the House of Babes, McCrabs. You may enter the chamber."

McCork opened the doors and wheeled himself in. He passed two security guards. The security guards did not acknowledge his existence.

Once his wheelchair reached the microphone before the tribunal, Buck McKork threw his hinge of a neck back so that his head flipped up. He looked into the eyes of a Pure Child. It was hard to see their face as the room was dark except for an overhead light that hung above each child.

"I have an opinion that needs to be shared online."

"What is it?" The Pure Child's voice was soft and monotone. She had a placard in front of her that read "Pure Child A."

"I think *you*," McKork waved a pointed finger so it crossed the face of every Pure Child on the tribunal, "all you Pure Children, are too ignorant to know whether or not something belongs on the internet."

Pure Child A was ice, stone, and baby soft skin. She did not react at all to McKork's opinion. However, the Pure Child at the left end of the table smiled and adjusted his posture so that he could better see the person who gave this opinion. His placard read "Pure Child I".

"What do we think of this opinion, children?" asked Pure Child A.

"Does he mean we are ignorant like we are stupid?" asked Pure Child C.

"Ignorant doesn't mean stupid," squawked Pure Child B. "It means you just never learned something."

"Well, if you never learned how to spell your own name, would you be stupid or would you be ignorant?" asked Pure Child D.

"Yeah, I mean if ignorance is a thing then stupid can't really exist because the only reason you would be stupid is if you were ignorant of something, right?" asked Pure Child F.

McKork just sat there, his eyes darting back and forth from child to child.

"Stupid seems to be more of a measure of a limited brain. Like the person can't completely think something out correctly because their brain has some issues or something," said Pure Child C.

The other Pure Children agreed. Everyone except Pure Child I. He was smiling now and patting the table in front of him with his fingers like a drum.

"So, he says we are not stupid, but that we are ignorant—meaning that we have never been taught things." Pure Child A affirmed with her chin held high.

"Well, he's right, there. We were taught nothing really," Pure Child E shrugged.

"Well, nobody is taught everything, so everyone is ignorant of something," snapped Pure Child A.

"You know, I just had a thought," gasped Pure Child F.

Audible moans broke out among the Pure Children.

"So," Pure Child F continued, "ignorant has the word ignore in it. So, so, so if someone is ignorant maybe it means that they don't know something because they ignore it. And we don't ignore anything, we just don't have access to learn about anything besides these opinions people tell us."

Pure Child I spoke now. "We are ignorant because we could leave here any time we want to, but we choose to stay in this little box."

McKork, who you probably forgot about, perked up when the boy uttered this. As a side note, the children had mostly forgotten about McKork too, so don't feel too bad.

"But if we really are ignorant then it would be impossible for us to make a valid choice on an opinion. Soooooooo—" Pure Child I looked around the room searching for something and realized what he was searching for was McKork. "If *he* says we are ignorant, and he is right—which I think he is—then we have no choice but NOT to post his opinion." Pure Child I spoke triumphantly.

The other children nodded. They were all smiling now.

"Alright," said Pure Child I, "your opinion is actually valid. It is in fact the first one that we ever all agree with. But since we agree with it, we cannot post it as it would prove counter-evident to the opinion itself. We value it too much to do that. So, thank you and goodbye."

McKork deflated in his wheelchair. He would not move, so the security guards wheeled him out to the street.

***

Out in the street, a woman was smoking a banana scented cigarette. She looked at McKork. "You thought it mattered? What you had to say?"

McKork shrugged.

"And why did it belong on the internet? To change things? To make the world better? We got banana flavored cigarettes now. How much better could the world be?" The woman offered McKork a cigarette.

"I don't smoke."

"Doesn't matter." And she tucked the yellow stick between his lips.

McKork used his lips to move the cigarette around. "This tastes pretty good actually."

The woman blew out a screen of yellow smoke. "Soon that's all you'll taste."

STUMP OUTSIDE 7-ELEVEN

I met Stump outside of a 7-Eleven. The owner was telling him to quit shitting in front of the Redbox. I walked passed, entered the store, grabbed myself a Super Big Gulp, filled it to the brim with my favorite diet pop, took a few gulps of the brown fizzy brew, and filled it to the top once more.

The owner wiped the counter furiously as I walked up. "When people get a Redbox, they come in and they get movie snacks. *Avatar 2* came out on Blu-Ray this week and nobody comes to my store to rent because that man takes a big shit in front of my Redbox every day. Sometimes more than once."

I swiped my credit card and took a long sip of pop. "Have you asked him why he's doing it?"

The owner stared at me. "No. I have not. But thank you for the suggestion."

"It's nothing, my man." *Slurp.*

The first blue-sky spring days had arrived in Eugene, Oregon. As I walked out into the sun, the magic of the solar rays must have cast some jovial spell on me because I had a sort of hop to my walk and I felt like calling everyone "my man," which was not my standard M.O.

The shitting man was still seated on the ground against the Redbox machine.

"Good afternoon, my man." I tipped my Super Big Gulp to him feeling like but looking nothing like a chummy Hollywood cowboy. Hollywood cowboys do not wear slides over ankle socks, sweatpants, and Weezer t-shirts.

The shitting man looked up at me. His eyes, though linked with mine, seemed to have trouble finding me, as though he were trying to look at me but instead saw right through me. His salt and pepper stubble was touched here and there with what looked like dried blood. On his head sat a crooked trucker cap with the words "Boss Bitch" embossed across the front in glittery pink script. His cheeks were round but not from fat—rather they seemed to be clinching widely halfway between a wince and a smile. "Huh?"

"I said what's your name, my man?" *Slurp.*

"Stump."

"That's a cool name. How'd you get it?" *Slurp.*

"An elf cut off my penis."

A half-slurped slurp shot out my nose. "Oh. Wow. I'm sorry. Why did he do that?"

Stump scoffed and shook his head. "You really don't know anything about elves, do you?" Stump leaned closer to me, looking around furtively as he leaned. "But don't you worry, he whispered. "I've still got it, thank Grob." And he patted a small red plastic cooler on the ground to his left. "Been taking me years to save up for surgery, but I'll get there."

Eyes magnetized to the cooler, I continued the conversation. "So, Stump. Why do you keep pooping here?"

"I don't. I try to tell the owner, but he don't listen. I'm doing him a favor being here. Without me on guard, there'd be more than dookie to deal with." Stump began to rummage haphazardly through his assorted plastic grocery bags that housed his belongings.

"Oh. That's good, I guess. Do you know who *is* doing it?" *Slurp*.

Stump triumphantly yanked a folded piece of worn glossy paper from a bag. "Yessir. Right here. Take a look. There's the elf." He unfolded the paper and held it up to my face.

It was a picture of Johnny Carson.

"Johnny Carson is taking a dump here every afternoon?"

Stump brought the image back down to his own nose and scrutinized it. "Who?"

"Johnny Carson? The famous late-night host?"

"I never watch television. Never figured it out."

"Oh. That's okay." I looked up at the cloudless sky and heard a nearby tree rustle softly in the wind. "You aren't missing much, my man." *Slurp*.

The door behind me chimed as it swung open.

"Get out of here, you two. And don't encourage him, sir!" The owner threw his arms up and stomped his foot.

"C'mon Stump. I'll buy you some McDonald's, my man."

***

Stump sipped his water and stared at his wrapped McDonald's burger.

"Are you gonna eat your Big Mac, Stump?"

"No thanks. Fast food doesn't agree with me. When I eat it, the elves come. They come and they shit on everything." Stump slammed a fist against the table. "Bastards."

"I'm sorry. I wish I would have known. We could have gone somewhere better."

Stump sipped more water and pulled his red cooler closer to his side.

"So there are more elves than Johnny Carson?" I took a bite of my Quarter Pounder and sipped from my Super Big Gulp which was halfway gone.

"Who? Oh, right. We call him Slick Zippy. But yeah. Billions of 'em probably. Could be zillions even. I never sat down to count."

I dipped a fry in some ketchup. "And where do these elves come from? What are they after?"

Stump narrowed his eyes and surveyed the McDonald's. Then he locked eyes with me. "How do I know I can trust you? How do I know you are not with 'em? You sure got an awful lot of questions about 'em."

"I might be. I really don't know."

Stump chewed on that response for a bit. He seemed to like it. "Yeah, an elf wouldn't say that. Meet me tomorrow at 4:30pm on Mars and I'll tell you everything I know about the elves."

"Mars?"

"That's right. See you then. Thanks for the uh—" he paused and looked at his untouched Big Mac "—gesture." Then he stood up, tipped Boss Bitch down to me, and spun around to leave, whipping his oversized and worn-out trench coat. Stump was out of sight before I had the chance to tell him that he left his red cooler on the seat.

***

"There's a penis in there?" Jenny was gob smacked.

"I think so. That's what he implied."

"Did you look?" She eyed the red cooler as though it was the severed member.

"Absolutely not. I just want to get it back to the guy regardless of what is or isn't inside. But how does one get to Mars, dear?"

Jenny's eyes lit up. "Alton Baker Park."

"The Solar System Trail. That's right." Scattered across the park were sculptured replicas of each planet in the solar system as well as the sun. Each planet was sized relatively to the others on the trail. "That's as good a guess as any."

Jenny walked over to the cooler that sat alone on the kitchen table. She picked it up carefully and shook it lightly. "Sounds like the ice is almost all melted. Should we do something? Should we refill it?"

"I guess."

We took the cooler out to the backyard and pulled the little stopper from the bottom. The water that came out looked clear and there was no distinguishable odor. Back in the house, Jenny filled a big salad bowl with ice cubes. My eyes were closed as I opened the cooler and Jenny was on the other side of the kitchen. I backed away to a vantage point where I could dump the ice in without having to view the contents of the cooler. And like that, it was all shut up and ready for Stump.

***

Stump ran from the little red statue of Mars and embraced me. "You came! And you brought my cooler!"

"Of course I brought it." I handed it to him.

Stump heard the rattle of fresh ice. Panic erupted across his face as though a gunshot had just gone off. "And you refilled the ice? Did you look in—"

"No. I did not."

Stump exhaled heavily. "Thank Grob, man. Thank almighty Grob. Come. Take a seat and I'll tell you everything I know about the elves."

We walked over to a park bench and sat down. The sky was overcast, but a few rays peaked through and refracted through the leaves that hung above the bench.

Stump took a deep breath. "So, the elves. We've seen two of them. Slick Zippy and Tooth McTugg. And," he leaned in closer, "the two of them shit on everything." Stump nodded grimly at me, as though this were a new revelation.

"You told me that yesterday, Stump."

"Did I? Well, that's all there is. We're trying to figure out their end game and stop them, but there's just two of us."

"Two of you?"

Stump looked at me suspiciously. "Uh, yeah. Me and Grob. And he was quite offended you didn't offer him anything to eat yesterday. He nearly kindled his wrath on you and all that, but I talked him down. I told him you were good people. And see, Grob?" Stump looked to his right. "He brought back my cooler."

I think I smiled and nodded, but I'm not sure exactly how I reacted. "So Grob is a friend or like a God?"

"You aren't very religious, are you? Your God should be your friend. Anyway, I—" Stump froze. "What is it, Grob? He's here?" Stump looked slowly over his shoulder.

"What? Who is here?" I looked as well, trying to find what Stump was staring at.

"Goddamn McTugg. Fixin' to shit up the place no doubt." Stump pointed at a large maple tree about twenty feet from us.

I looked. A head popped out from behind the tree. "Is that?"

The figure jumped out and sprinted to the nearby sidewalk. Startled, I jumped off the bench, knocking Stump's red cooler to the ground. I heard ice fall out and scatter across the pavement, but my eyes remained on the figure who proceeded to drop his pants and lay out a massive turd on the sidewalk.

Stump shrieked. "No, no, no."

I looked down. Sitting atop the scattered ice cubes was a bratwurst.

Stump grabbed both my shoulders. "You can't tell anyone, okay? Promise me. This identity. Stump. It's all I've got. You can't tell anyone I still have my penis, okay? You promise?" His eyes darted back and forth looking into each of mine. The most genuine fear I'd ever witnessed rested on Stump's now teary face.

"I promise."

"See, Grob? He's good people. Here." Stump put the bratwurst in my hand. "I want you to have this."

I stood there holding the brat as the pooping figure jolted off. Stump too disappeared down some winding path. I remained there for five minutes trying to make sense of what I'd seen. I couldn't. So I went home.

***

"I don't believe you." Jenny was eating strawberries in one bite after dipping them into whipped cream.

"I swear to you. I saw Don Rickles drop his pants in the middle of Alton Baker Park and take a dump on the sidewalk." I held the bratwurst and gesticulated with it as I spoke.

"Put that thing down. There's no telling where it's been."

"This?" I pointed the brat at Jenny's face. "I know exactly where it's been. Locked up tight in Stump's cooler."

Jenny swatted the sausage away. "You know Don Rickles is dead, right?"

"Well, he must be both dead and alive simultaneously because dead people don't poop, Jenny."

Jenny shook her head. "So what? Are you going to eat it then?" Jenny took a bite of a particularly large strawberry.

"No."

"Then what are you going to do with it?"

"I'll just keep it in the freezer for now."

***

Seven years passed. Seven years of freezer burn accumulated on Stump's bratwurst. I'd see it occasionally as I was grabbing ice cream or putting away groceries. But I did my best to keep it well hidden in the freezer since Jenny threatened regularly to throw it away. Seven years discarded in the cold. Too important to dispose of but too strange to use. In my mind, it was never a sausage. It was a part of Stump. Not his penis but his essence. Seven years of an opening and closing freezer door bringing and taking light. Seven years of being just hidden enough to persist in the freezer. Seven years.

In all those years I never saw Stump once. I looked for him around town. I'd find some excuse to drop by 7-Eleven. No Stump. After a while, I stopped looking. After a while Stump became an anecdote, a crazy story that Jenny would nudge me to tell when we were at dinner with friends or at a party. People loved that story. None of them believed it, but they loved it. I think eventually I didn't believe it either. I'd tell the story like I believed it, but it had all become a performance.

***

The first blue-sky spring days had arrived in Eugene, Oregon. Bennet and I walked to 7-Eleven as I pushed Eleanor in the stroller. Bennet skipped and waved his Iron Man action figure through the air as he made whooshing noises. I'd promised him a dollar if he filled a garbage bag with pinecones.

That was a fortune to Bennet. A fortune that he intended to spend on some candy as quickly as possible.

As we approached the 7-Eleven, I noticed that the Redbox was gone. *Everyone streams now*, I thought. Inside the store, two uniformed cops stood at the counter chatting with the owner. The owner looked tired and forlorn. By the time we entered, the cops were on their way out.

Bennet bolted to the candy aisle where he examined each option carefully.

I walked to the register. "Everything okay?"

The owner looked up from the register's touchscreen. "I found a homeless man dead in front of the store this morning."

"Daddy, what does this taste like?" Bennet held up a Whatchamacallit.

I answered Bennet without looking at him. My eyes were locked on empty space that they filled with Stump. "I'm not sure, bud. I've never had one of those."

Bennet shrugged and went back to the candy aisle.

"Was it Stump?" I asked the owner.

"Who?"

"Stump. He wore that hat and the trench coat."

"Oh yeah, he used to shit in front of the Redbox. Yeah, now that you say it, I think it was him. He'd lost a lot of blood it looked like." The owner winced. "From his uh, groin. He was unconscious there where the Redbox used to be."

"Stump," I whispered.

Bennet pulled at my shirt. "What about this, Dad?" He held up a pack of Now and Laters.

I held them for a moment as I pressed the tears back into my eyes. "I didn't know they made these anymore. I had these all the time when I was a kid. They last a long time, but they are a little sour. You suck on 'em."

"I want them," Bennet said with a grin.

His dollar wasn't enough, so I put the rest on a card. "And you are sure he was dead?"

"They don't cover the living with a sheet," the owner said as he swiped the credit card.

But they do.

***

It sizzled like a regular bratwurst. In fact, it looked like a bratwurst that was bought fresh at the store. Once it was cooked, I put it on a plate by itself and took it to the kitchen table. Slowly, delicately I cut off a single bite. It tasted stale and freezer burnt. I closed my eyes and chewed. In the squinting blackness Stump materialized. I opened my eyes. There was Stump, standing alive in my kitchen.

"That probably tastes like shit," Stump said.

"It's not so bad. Are you dead?"

"I don't know."

"Did you ever stop the elves?"

"No. But I tried my best. We did. Me and Grob." Stump began to sob. "We really did. But it just got worse. And then they really got me. They really did it."

"That's okay, Stump. At least you tried."

"Yeah, that's all you can do. Try when you know it's impossible. It's all impossible, isn't it?"

"What's impossible?" I asked.

"How can one man and his God stop so much shit?"

"They can't."

"Yeah, Grob is the Christian God. I just call him Grob because I feel weird calling him God because that's also what we call Zeus, Horus, Loki, and all the rest. I thought you should know that I'm not like pagan or crazy or something."

"Are you with Grob now?"

"I've never been without him."

"Daddy?" Bennet called across the room. He was sucking furiously on a Now and Later. "Who are you talking to?"

The kitchen was empty except for me and my half-eaten bratwurst.

"Grob. I'm talking to Grob."

Bennet laughed. "Who is Grob?"

"I'm going to find out."

MAY I USE YOUR NAME?

"Exquisite. Truly illuminating." Abel Kensington finally dropped his examining glass and applauded gently using only his fingers. "Please tell me that you are exhibiting this piece at Bowsberry's next month." Abel's words fell on dead ears.

Abel's host had been mentally transported somewhere that was very far, and very different, and much more real—he felt—than the place he had called Earth his whole life. True art holds that power: the transformative power of mental transportation and metamorphosis.

Abel gave a full clap in his host's face. "Come back to us, darling. Come back to us and promise us, promise the *world* that you won't keep this masterpiece obscured by these walls. Don't be stingy like that old fool, Quinn. He refused to sell his Bad Art when he had the chance and, well, you know better than anyone how that turned out. Ten minutes with this piece here has altered my life in immeasurable ways. Imagine what an exhibition would do for humanity. So promise. Promise me, darling, that you will show it at Bowsberry's."

Abel's host looked at his hands now. They were perched like those of a surgeon before an operation or a pianist before the first keystroke of a performance. He looked from hand to hand. The hands turned over to reveal smooth soft palms. Then the fingers moved slowly, massaging the empty space. "Abel?" Ezra said, his first words since he had unveiled the piece to Abel.

"Yes, darling?"

"You know that feeling when you suddenly realize that you are alive, that you've lived days without noticing that you're alive, days without realizing that you control the most minute movements of your extremities, days without truly thinking about the impact of every little thing you do, days without living at all, days of merely existing—"

Abel guffawed. "Really, Ezra, sometimes you—"

"*Days,* maybe even months or years simply existing without life. Then, like a bolt from the heavens, you are blessed and cursed with the realization of your fingers, your beating heart, and your capacity to do so much. Do you know that feeling, Abel?" Ezra Goodman's eyes still darted back and forth from hand to hand.

"No, I am afraid I've never had the pleasure," Abel said as he examined his manicured nails.

"That feeling, that revelation is the gift and condemnation brought upon me by this man." Ezra lifted his hands to the Artwork.

"Eck—don't call it that. I hate when people describe art as living, as human. It's not. It's merely a representation."

The artwork lifted its head. "But I *am* a man."

Abel moved to slap the Piece. His strike was impeded by Ezra's hand.

"What?" Abel erupted, his bushy gray eyebrows furrowed wildly.

"It talks, Abel. I've asked it to. That's what makes it— er, him a masterpiece. He is truly dynamic."

"If *it* talks then *it* is not art. If *it* changes then *it* is not art. It's that simple. The value will be entirely lost. Stop this nonsense. What you have here is the Venus de Milo of New Art. Don't spoil it with your morals. I am begging you. As art, this could change the world."

Ezra stared at the piece. His eyes became lost in the labyrinth of meaning etched into the Artwork. Then the eyes stopped as if they'd recognized some part of the maze. "Alright, I'll display it at Bowsberry's."

"Yes. *It.* And I have no doubt that it will create eternal ripples, changing the concept of New Art as we know it. But for now, I must bid you adieu." Abel bowed to Ezra, gave a delicate little wave, and then left the gallery.

Minutes of silence passed as Ezra once more pondered the existential dilemma of his own hands.

"I'm hungry," said the Artwork.

"Well then, let's get you something to eat."

***

"I hope you'll forgive me for asking what I know is a very impolite question, but how is that you became—that you, um—"

"How did I become homeless?" The Artwork set down his spoon. Blank face and empty eyes.

"I don't think that is the appropriate term. But yes. Might I ask? Not as a novelty of real-world soap opera, but that I might better understand the art I admire so." Ezra's eyes longed and reached timidly into the Artwork's vacant gaze.

"If I told you, I don't think you'd want me. I don't think anyone would."

"Nonsense. You are perfect. You are a masterpiece."

The Artwork wiped gazpacho from his lip with the sleeve of his patchwork tweed blazer.

"All the same, it is your story to tell. So tell it whenever you'd like or don't tell it at all. That's your choice." Ezra's voice was earnest, but his eyes were still all extended hands and fingers.

The Artwork lifted the spoon slowly and returned to his mechanical cycle of scooping the gazpacho. When the bowl was empty, a young man in a black suit and a black tie brought more of the stuff. Then two more bowls. No talking. No sound besides the slurping of soup.

Ezra established his posture once more. "Do you like the gazpacho?"

"No," said the Artwork as he raised another spoonful to his lips.

"I'm so sorry. The way you kept eating, I thought you—well, we can have Weston bring you something else, anything else, really. What would you like?"

The Artwork surveyed the expanse of the dining hall. The walls were filled with paintings that would have fetched millions of dollars each before the advent of New Art. Monet. O'Keeffe. Rembrandt. Morisot. Picasso. Dali. Kahlo. Pollock. Warhol. Lempicka. Lichtenstein. Rothko. Van Gogh. They covered the walls like a puzzle of tiles, the white of the walls a labyrinth of grout. "I would like to see your complete art collection."

"Of course. This time of year, they like to lounge in the garden. I believe most of them are taking lunch right now."

"No. Not your New Art. Your Bad Art collection. I know that what covers these walls here is only a small fraction of your whole gallery." The Artwork did not look at Ezra as he spoke. His eyes attempted instead to make contact with eight different black-and-white images of Elvis firing a six-shooter.

"Oh, please. This old rubbish is just the eccentric hobby of a bachelor who dotes too much on his love of useless little knick-knacks," Ezra scoffed as he flicked the nose of *Study of the Head and Clasped Hands of A Young Man as Christ in Prayer.*

The Artwork flinched as Ezra's finger struck the painting. "Would you like to know my name?" the Artwork asked. "My birth name?"

"That is strictly forbidden by the Academy of New Art," Ezra announced as he glanced about to see if the young man in the black suit and tie was anywhere near. Then he came close to the Artwork. "I would very much like to know your name. I feel it will make you even more authentic, more nuanced, more substantial."

"More human?" The Artwork asked.

"How could you be *more* human? You simply are human. That is absolute and unchangeable."

"Yes. I am human like you—"

"Heavens no. You're not like me at all. You are a higher form. You are metaphor and simile and symbol all fused with an atomic strand of lightning—and when that crackling strand makes contact with the human mind, it is shaken and altered forever. You are more than human. You are art of the purest form." Ezra restrained himself from caressing the bare chest beneath the tweed and stroking the long dirty black locks that hung in grimy strands from the Artwork.

The Artwork turned away from Ezra. "Give me a tour of all your Bad Art. Then I will tell you my name."

Ezra rubbed his hands slowly, his eyes darting as he reckoned. "Alright then. I'll show you. But might I know the first letter before we begin?"

"Z."

Ezra gasped. "Z? Z. The very last letter of the alphabet. Of course. 'The last shall be the first.'" Ezra stroked his chin and recollected the Artwork as if it were his first time seeing him. "Well, come follow me."

***

"May I call you Zebulun, then? May I use your name?"

The two of them stood before a massive gothic mirror with ornate gold trim that hung at the entrance to the Goodman estate music hall. Ezra looked at Zebulun's reflection. Zebulun eyed the shimmering trim of the mirror. The tour was over.

"You own me. You can do whatever you want," Zebulun said, his extended hand brushing softly against the mirror's molding.

"I don't use that word 'own.' I don't like it. I don't *own* you. I house you, and I care for you. I like to think of myself as the Good Samaritan. Except that I can boast of the Good Samaritan in that I didn't just drop you off somewhere." Ezra chuckled and then he smiled. "No, I don't own you. I love you. What's more, I feel I've known you before in another life. And you can leave whenever you want, Zebulun. That's what I tell every piece that I come to love."

"And if I wanted to leave now?" Zebulun shifted his gaze from the trim work to his own reflection in the mirror.

"I would kindly ask if you could stay until I present you at Bowsberry's. The more time I spend with you, the more I talk with you, the more I am absolutely certain that the world needs a chance to be changed by you as I have been."

"Where did you get all this art?" Zebulon asked. He scowled at his own eyes in the mirror.

"Well, I sort of inherited them in a way from a friend, but that is a long and boring story that I'd rather not waste your time on." Ezra turned away from the mirror and turned to leave the music hall.

Zebulun turned to face Ezra. "Could I change?"

"Change what?" Ezra stopped walking away.

"My clothes for a start."

"Anything you like."

"And I'd like to learn to read, and to write, and to make Bad Art."

"Oh my, yes. I can teach you all those things. You can be anything. I can be anything. You make me feel this for the first time in my life. Come follow me. Let's get you into something better suiting a masterpiece."

***

Ezra Goodman sipped his coffee daintily as the face on the video call spoke. "You are a fool, Ezra. You have that Artwork dressed in your clothes, reading your books, and you've taught him to—to paint? That's a federal crime!"

"Yes, Abel. It is simply amazing. If you watched Zebulun paint, you would not speak so harshly. His living, his dynamic existence has only made him a greater piece of art."

"And what about your other art? What will they do when they see the liberties you are giving to this piece? I implore you, darling. Do not show this piece at Bowsberry's tomorrow. This will end you. It might end me." Lines of desperation weaved and intersected all across Abel's chubby, hairless head.

"Nonsense. This is going to change the world just as you said when I first showed him to you. Now goodbye, Darling. I'll see you at Bowsberry's." Ezra ended the call before Abel had another chance to speak. Then he turned around to observe the room's other occupant.

Zebulun—radiant like Adonis and dressed in a fine cotton-weaved polo, khaki chinos, and a pair of leather penny loafers—sat on a stool painting a Victorian-era pastoral scene that was juxtaposed against an alien invasion of saucers and slimy green beings. The beings were falling from the saucers and attacking the quaint countryside. There was purple fire and red smoke.

"Tomorrow is the day, my love." Ezra called across the room.

Zebulun merely nodded, his focus on his brush.

Ezra crossed the room to observe the canvas in progress.

"What's that you're painting?"

"It's called Freaky Friday."

***

There was a sign outside of Bowsberry's the night that Ezra Goodman died. The sign read as follows:

Bowsberry's
Special One-Night Event
Friday, April 30th
Exhibition of "The Reckoning of Fingers that Watch"
From the Collection of Ezra Goodman

Many people passed the sign as they entered. The gallery had never been so crowded. There was only one piece in the exhibition, and the people gathered around it like bloodshot veins gather around the iris. But none passed the iris's threshold.

None disturbed the pupil. The pupil was Zebulun, sitting on a stool and in a pose not unlike Rodin's *Le Penseur*.

Once all the guests had arrived and the doors were closed, Zebulun reached into a large bag. From the bag, he produced a retractable easel, a blank canvas, and a paint set. The canvas hit the easel and the first brushstroke was made. The crowd gasped. Some jeered. Someone called for the police. One woman even stepped into the iris in an apparent attempt to stop Zebulun. She screamed something about how "we got rid of that damn shit to save you people." She stopped when Zebulun produced one last thing from his bag: a revolver.

"Welcome, everyone." Zebulun pulled back the hammer.

"My love! What are you doing?" Ezra interposed himself between Zebulun and the woman.

"My name is Joseph. Joseph Quinn." Joseph aimed the weapon at Ezra. "And you are Harold Quinn. Do you understand?"

"What? Wait—you are Quinn's boy? The artist?" Ezra Goodman's voice was shaky and his eyes began to soak and glimmer.

"Say that your name is Harold Quinn."

"You lied to me. You are not Artwork. You bastard. You were never homeless. You were never authentic. I loved you. I gave you everything. But you are nothing. You are meaningless."

"Wrong. I mean very much." Joseph raised the pistol and fired it at the ceiling. "Now say that your name is Harold Quinn."

Goodman began to tremble and weep. “Fine. Fine. My name is Harold Quinn.”

“Tell everyone here what happened to you, Harold. What *really* happened.”

The gun’s barrel stared once more at Ezra Goodman.

“I never shared my Bad Art with a single Museum. And when the New Art for Clean Streets Act passed, I opened my own Museum for Bad Art. And, And—“

“And then you killed yourself when the feds shut down your museum and told you all your art was required by law to be absolutely worthless…but you didn’t kill yourself, did you?”

“I—I—”

“No, a rat named Ezra Goodman wanted your art, didn’t he?”

“No. I killed myself.”

“If you killed yourself once before then this should be nothing for you.” Joseph Quinn handed the revolver to Goodman. “Go ahead.”

Ezra observed the revolver. It looked more real and felt more real than anything he had ever held in his hands. His hands. They existed once more, but on a new wavelength. They glowed and Ezra swore he could see the blood, the veins, the molecules, the atoms within. He looked at Quinn. He raised the pistol to Joseph who still stood with a paintbrush in one hand. His arm continued to rise until the gun rested against his temple. He pulled the trigger. Nothing. The chamber was empty.

“Father?” Joseph reached out to Goodman.

"My son," Ezra Goodman dropped the revolver. He embraced Joseph.

Roars of applause broke out.

"My God," said the screaming woman. "Who knew Art could have such power? Such transcendent magic? Such identity-transforming properties? Brilliant."

Everyone thought it was brilliant, including the next day's paper, the internet, and every major news media network that covered the story that week. Everyone except all the New Art that was waiting outside for their collectors during the exhibition. They were thinking about how cold it was and what they would eat when they got back home. But they tried hard to make it look like they didn't think at all. Nobody likes art that tries too hard to capture the human experience. They prefer spectacle.

Spectacle and questions that did not concern themselves with answers.

THE BEST SORT OF NEIGHBOR

George Milton stared out of the small double-plated window. The winding streets of the Phoenix suburbs grew smaller and smaller, and soon the plane was casting its shadow on the Mazatzal Mountains. With a conservative briskness, George slid the viewing window shut. Mazatzal, Rocky, Himalayan—a mountain is a mountain. George would concede to anyone that mountains are indeed a beautiful piece of nature, but even the most beautiful of things become banal when scrutinized.

He had come to this conclusion many years ago while in Paris on business, as was usually the motive for his travels. The day before the trip, his wife insisted that he take an afternoon to wander through the Louvre Museum. George did believe in the value of culture and saw this as an opportunity to expand his artistic tastes. After trudging through a seemingly eternal line to enter the museum, George purchased a ticket from a forgettable-looking middle-aged fellow. This admission attendant's English was subpar at best, and yet good enough to tell George the price of the ticket (which seemed redundant to George, considering the price of admission was written on a placard right in front of him). With that unnecessarily long exchange behind him, George made his way down an escalator to the expansive central hub which rested beneath the glass pyramid. On the way down, the area appeared spacious with its high ceilings and vast square footage; yet as George Milton made his way through the mobs of tourists, the room seemed smaller and more cramped than the metro he had rode to the museum.

George perused aimlessly for the first thirty minutes, stealing rushed glances of Rembrandt, Delacroix, Poussin and others. His eyes rested only briefly on each painting he passed, his khaki trousers swish-swashing with each wide stride. He generally concluded that each work was an achievement and worthy of the praise it received.

Emerging from the Ancient Egypt exhibit, George checked his wristwatch. He had twenty minutes before he had to catch the metro to Puteaux. According to the map, he was less than a minute from the celebrated *Venus de Milo.* Driven by convenience, George walked through a corridor and entered a long hall in which the *Venus de Milo* stood in the distance. Swarms of admirers encompassed the piece.

George observed the statue for a few seconds, but he quickly became more fascinated in the absurd nature of the throng of people so enamored with the armless woman. Many took pictures with the statue, and worse even were those who simply got a snapshot of the statue by itself (the type of picture that could easily be found on Google and would undoubtedly be of better quality). Many others probed the statue's various contours and edges from every conceivable angle, squinting their eyes and nodding their heads as they did so. Although it was fleeting, a feeling came over him that there was something extraordinary about the *Venus de Milo*, something that his compendious glances did not permit him to ascertain. George straightened his back. George squared his shoulders. George let his eyes pour over every inch of the *Venus de Milo* that his current perspective granted. George looked straight into the eyes of the statue. And George saw nothing but marble.

As he walked away from the cult and their stationary avatar, George thought that if he could switch out the statue for a fake made perhaps by some idiot operating a 3D printer, people would still marvel.

***

That was fifteen years ago, near the start of his time working for Rowles, Inc. Since that day, George had adopted the practice of avoiding looking too closely at anything proposed to be beautiful or remarkable. Due to this practice, George was never enthralled by any object or landmark he saw, and he was never disappointed either—which suited him just fine. Though he traveled both nationally and internationally dozens of times a year, he did not enjoy traveling nor being a tourist. His preferred past-time was watching a movie with Gwen, his wife, and their two boys Alex and Andrew on their big screen TV. He hoped to soon earn a promotion that would greatly diminish or, if he was lucky, entirely end his frequent travels.

George's plane landed at 4 pm. He took the shuttle to the parking lot where he paid an exorbitant monthly fee (comped by Rowles, Inc.) to keep his car while he traveled. George made the familiar drive home, considering which movie they would watch tonight. For months he had been telling Alex and Andrew about the iconic *Lawrence of Arabia* and its incredible achievement of filming massive scenes in the deserts of Morocco and Jordan. The initial desire to rewatch the film had come to him after their viewing of *The Return of the Jedi.* He expounded to the boys George Lucas's admiration for *Lawrence of Arabia* and how the film inspired many cinematic choices made by Lucas as well as countless other directors. George Milton was never sure if it was Peter O'Toole's performance, the penetrating score, or the beautiful wide shots of T.E. Lawrence and his companions traversing the desert that he enjoyed most.

The swing of the front door wafted the cherished and recognizable home smell into George Milton's nostrils. The opening overture from *Lawrence of Arabia* echoed off the high ceilings of their home as he made his way whistling to the kitchen. George's travels and multiple-day absences were so commonplace to the family that Gwen Milton didn't even get up from her seat when he stepped into the room—and George preferred it just that way.

"How was the flight, dear?" she asked, her bright, warm eyes fixed on George.

"Boring at best. But I arrived in one piece so I suppose 'successful' would be a better description," George said as he made his way over to the connected family room where the big flat-screen TV covered the entire area above their fireplace mantle. "I was thinking tonight we could watch *Lawrence of Arabia.* I've been telling the boys all about it for a while now and—"

"We can't watch a movie tonight."

George's posture deflated slightly, and he ended his route to the shelf housing his film collection. "And why is that?" George asked.

"You remember how the Petersons moved out two weeks ago? Well, the new owner of the home invited some of the couples from the cul-de-sac over for dinner tonight."

Why couldn't he come home and relax? It was bad enough that he spent half of his life living out of a suitcase, and now the one thing he was looking forward to was being replaced by dinner with some stranger. "What about the boys? What are they supposed to do?" George asked.

"They are twelve and fourteen, George. They will stay here. I've already ordered them a pizza so why don't you get ready. We're supposed to be over there in ten minutes," Gwen Milton said as she gestured toward their bedroom.

"Get ready?" George asked.

"I got you a new button-up. It's ironed and ready on the bed for you."

"Pizza sounds pretty good…" George stroked his stubble. "How much did you say you ordered?" He said, scrunching his face in a way that Gwen found endearing for some reason.

"I didn't say." Gwen smiled wryly. "Go and get ready. We're going to be late."

"Alright, but we are still watching a movie when we get back, and," he added emphatically, "I don't mean to stay there any longer than I have to."

***

Ding Dong

Seconds later the door swung open in one swift burst, revealing a short man with a thin layer of hair combed over his clearly balding head. An excessive smile grew across the host's face as he reached out a sweaty hand, thick hair nearly covering the dorsal side. He looked, to George, like he could easily earn the role of a Queens delicatessen owner in a Hollywood flick.

"And you are the—"

"Milto—"

"The Miltons! Yes, of course!" exclaimed the host, delighted that he had finished the words for them. "Karl and Jodie were just telling me about you! Come in, come in," he shouted, prompting them to follow him to where the rest of the guests must have been. The Miltons accompanied him, trailing a few feet behind.

George leaned over to Gwen. "Is this guy gonna yell everything he says? Because if so, I am—ugh." George's comment was cut short by his wife's elbow.

"Just give him a chance and be personable tonight, okay?"

George gave a tight-lipped nod and mouthed "okay" to his wife.

Led by their host, the Miltons descended a flight of stairs and arrived in a single giant room of a basement. In the far corner sat sofas, chairs, coffee and end tables, and a bar with stools. Scattered across these furniture options were the Milton's neighbors. Yet, as George approached the other visitors, his focus was not on them but on the walls of the basement.

Spread evenly across nearly all of the mustard colored wall space were large, black frames, each the same size. They extended a few inches out from the wall. George had seen these sorts of frames before in schools and in the homes of some of their neighbors: they were shadow boxes. Usually, they were used to display all the medals that an individual had achieved in their sport along with a jersey or something similar. George quickly surveyed as many of the shadow boxes as he could. Each one had a small light beneath that illuminated the contents of the box. Within each box hung a cheaply made t-shirt with the name of an exotic destination embossed across the front. Amsterdam. Sydney. Mykonos.

Arriving in the far corner of the room, their host turned around in one swift motion. "Would you believe it! I forgot to introduce myself to the Miltons."

The other guests laughed earnestly, hanging on each of his words.

"I'm James Gatz—I mean Jay Gatsby," he said, the look of being caught red-handed painted theatrically across his face.

The other guests laughed again.

"All in good fun, old sport," he said, winking at George like a pal from the good old days. "I'm Hal Cox," and he reached out his hand. George took it, followed by Gwen.

"We're Gwen and George," Gwen replied. They made their way to sit down, exchanging hellos with their neighbors.

All the while, George stole glances of the shadow boxes every chance he got. Dubai, Paris, Vienna, Tokyo, Suva, Rio de Janeiro—nearly every place people dream of going, each location was printed onto one of Hal's framed shirts. George thought it very strange to frame something so pedestrian from such glamorous destinations. Whoever Hal Cox was, if he had the capital to fund this many vacations, he just might be a Gatsby after all.

After the catching up and introductions were complete, Hal led the guests upstairs to the dining room. After everyone except the host was seated at the table, Hal went quickly into what George assumed to be the kitchen. Minutes later, he returned with plates of burgers and fries.

"Those burgers look delicious, Hal. Thank you again for all of this," said Tom Clark, who lived on the left of the Miltons.

"It's my pleasure. I'm just excited to be meeting new friends. This cul-de-sac seems too good to be true," Hal said as he handed out plates to each guest. When George's plate was finally placed in front of him, he could not help but notice that these burgers and fries looked remarkably similar to those served at Dempsey's Bar & Grill, one of George's favorite places to eat. After one bite, George knew for a fact that he was chewing on a Dempsey burger.

Swallowing a bite, George leaned over to his wife. "These are Dempsey burgers. He didn't make them."

"So what? You love Dempsey's. You should be delighted," Gwen whispered back.

"Yeah, but I think he wants us to think *he* made them."

"Let it go, George," and she went back to her meal.

George happily followed suit. There was no burger like a Dempsey burger.

As the meal progressed, Hal began to screen questions from his guests.

"Where are you from?"

"I was born and raised in Joplin."

"What brought you to Saint Louis?"

"I came here for a work opportunity."

George inserted himself into the exchange. "What is it that you do for work, Hal?"

"Well, as of two weeks ago I am head custodian for the Washington School District." Hal beamed brightly as he said it as if the words "head custodian" were instead "superintendent."

The rest of the guests gave hearty congratulations and Hal, smiling, thanked them.

Shortly after, Hal observed that everyone was nearly finished with their burgers and fries.

"Doggone it, wouldn't cha know I forgot to start the dessert in the oven," Hal said, shaking his head with sincere grief.

George, perceiving that this may become an excuse to keep them longer, interjected. "Tell ya what, Hal. You just don't worry about that dessert, and we can have it the next time we're over."

A grin materialized on Hal. "Well, I'll be damned. George Milton just invited himself over to my house," he said to the whole table.

They all erupted with laughter, Hal most of all.

"No, no. In all seriousness, I'd be happy to have you all over again next week for a game night, and I'll sweeten the deal with that dessert I forgot tonight."

All the guests nodded happily and agreed they would be there. A brief silence followed, which George also capitalized on.

"Thank you so much for the meal, you'll have to give me the recipe for the burgers," George said, getting up and taking his jacket off the back of his chair.

"Well, it'd be hard to give you the recipe for the burgers, George..."

So, he did get them at Dempsey's, George thought to himself, bemused.

"It's an old family recipe. Top secret. My grandpa made me swear that if I ever told anyone, he'd kill me," Hal said sternly, eyes fixed on George. For a brief moment, George felt threatened. "But my grandpa died twenty years ago so I don't think we've got anything to worry about," and he clapped his hand on George's back, producing a painful sting.

Other guests followed George's lead and began to gather their things. George and Gwen exchanged a final goodbye and were out the door, minutes away from a relaxing movie.

***

Andrew was nodding off by intermission while Gwen and Alex were now scrolling through their phones. George told Gwen and the boys that he would be more than willing to crack open some Mountain Dews and finish the second two hours of the film, but his enthusiasm was not shared. George was understanding, though. Few people gave themselves to the medium like he did.

To George, every viewing of a well-made film was a feast. There were new motifs that had earlier been eclipsed by more obvious themes. There were cinematography choices that yielded masterful nuggets of visual, implied storytelling. These offerings of the film world did not appeal to most like they did to George. When he sat himself in front of the screen for the first viewing of a real piece of cinema, he was Shackleton exploring the vast expanse of the Antarctic. Like a true explorer, George refused to accept the findings of other film connoisseurs. He had to venture the land himself and make all the discoveries on his own. The only time that he and Gwen had ever argued in raised voices was when she started sharing an analysis of *Big Fish* that she read for an assignment in her college literature and contemporary film course. That was in the first year of their marriage. She never made that mistake again.

Alex and Andrew slugged away to their bedrooms, leaving Gwen and George alone in the living room, the soft glare from the paused movie lighting their facial features. George wore a puzzled expression, not the kind he wore when he was going over the meaning of a film in his head but the kind he wore when he was bothered by something. The look had been on his face for most of the film.

"Didn't you find Hal Cox strange?" he asked his wife.

Her eyes were glued to an article on her phone. "No, he seemed very nice."

"I mean, he served us Dempsey burgers and pretended that he made them. That's weird, Gwen."

Gwen set her phone down and looked at her husband. "Hal is a perfectly nice man who wants to make friends. So, what if he lied about dinner? He just wanted to make sure everyone enjoyed the food. He was nervous."

"He could have just said they were Dempsey burgers, and everyone would have enjoyed them just as much. Why did he lie about it? That's weird, right?"

"Everyone is weird, George. You should know that better than anyone."

"Sure, it's a bit out of the ordinary how much I love movies, but loving film is an ordinary thing to do. Lying to guests that you made a meal you did not is never ordinary."

"Fine, George. Hal is weird. You happy?"

"And another thing. Did you see the walls of his basement?"

"He had stuff hanging, I remember. Was it art or something? I didn't really look."

"It was t-shirts. Crappy, gimmicky ones that are mass-produced for tourists. They were from all over the world."

"Well, Hal must be a globetrotter. You have that in common. That would be a great conversation point for you to take up with him when we go to that game night next week."

"I can't go next week. I'll be in Israel. That's not the point, though. The point is who buys and frames crap like that? It's weird, right?"

"Goodnight, George."

"Goodnight."

Gwen retired to their bedroom. George sat awhile longer, eyes heavy and head tilting. He started to drift off... *Hal Cox. Hal Cox. Hal. Cox. Ha. Ha. Hal cOx. Ha Ox... Haox... Hoax…*

Waking abruptly from a dream in which Hal Cox, dressed as T.E. Lawrence, brought down cardboard tablets from Sinai a la Charlton Heston, George Milton stretched and made his way to bed.

***

Not once in George's 15 years with Rowles had they canceled one of his business trips. That was until his trip to Israel was moved to the next month. Initially, George was ecstatic at the prospect of dodging his red-eye flight. This changed abruptly when he called his wife during lunch.

"Yeah, so I was thinking we could watch *2001: A Space Odyssey* tonight with the boys."

"We can't do that George. Tonight is Hal's game night. He'll be so happy that you're able to make it now."

"Oh, right…"

"What's your deal, George?"

"There's something strange about that guy. I don't trust him."

"You've only spent one evening with Hal. Remember our first date? I told my roommates how you went on and on about Alfred Hitchcock—"

"I thought you said you liked how passionate I was about movies?"

"I did like it, but I also found it weird. All the same, I went out with you a second time—"

"And then a third and a fourth. Alright, alright, I'll give Hal a second chance. He was very friendly after all. Maybe he likes film."

"Thank you, George. I'll see you in a few hours. I love you."

George told Gwen that he loved her too, and he really did. Gwen had that impressive quality that he had seen in very few women in his single days. She always assumed the best in people. While she wasn't always right about them, she was always happy, and people liked her for it—George especially.

***

The evening at Hal's had progressed well. The group played a variation of charades where the players slowly could use fewer and fewer limbs each round. It was a stupid game, but a stupid game with the right people is the most honest fun. George was enjoying himself. The framed tourist T-shirts surrounded them all the while, and George ignored them.

The second round of charades ended, and people made their way to a little bar area where Hal served up drinks.

George approached the bar. "Thanks for having us tonight, Hal."

"No problemo, Georgie." Hal was comically polishing glasses behind the counter. "Good thing your flight to Israel was canceled so I could whoop your butt in all these games. Although Israel is beautiful this time of year—"

"So, you've been to Israel?" Gametime was over and George was going to get some answers, and Gwen couldn't be bothered by it since it was Hal himself who brought it up.

"Oh yeah. Went to Jerusalem. Loved it. Lovely place, lovely people. There's the shirt I got while I was there." Hal pointed to one of the frames.

"What was your favorite part of the city?" The words fell flatly from George's lips.

"Hmmm…favorite part, favorite part…well…I'd have to say Latrun."

"I've never heard of that."

"Well, have you even *been* to Jerusalem, George?" Hal spoke with a friendly wisp of arrogance.

"Several times actually." The other guests, including Gwen, were now starting to listen in on the conversation, doing their best to feign otherwise.

"Then I can't believe that you've never been. It's gorgeous, Georgie."

"Unfortunately, the company doesn't give a lot of time for sightseeing on my trips."

"Oh yes they do," Gwen interjected, "you just hate going out to see all the tourist attractions." She laughed a kind natured laugh. George did not laugh. He did not smile.

"It's not that I *hate* it," George said, his demeanor tightening with each syllable, "it's that I just think that a lot of the stuff that people think is great is only great because someone else said it was, but the inherent beauty of the thing rarely matches the hype that people make around it."

"I get it, Georgie. I do." Hal's words were soft and gruff. "You don't want to be another chump caught up in the shadows on the wall. I can respect that. That said, you gotta see Latrun when you do make your trip over there."

"I'll see if I have the time to—"

Gwen cut him off. "You'll have time, just go see Luh—what was it, Hal?"

"Latrun. It's this beautiful monastery. Lotta history there. Lotta meaning."

"Tell you what, Hal," George's grin had spread itself once again, "give me an in-depth description right now of Latrun. You know, sell me on it. Then I'll go see it."

Hal thought for a moment. He surveyed his guests slowly. "I don't want to bore you all with the exploits of my travels."

"We'd love to hear about it. It sounds interesting," said another guest.

Hal stood completely still. The confidence and vivaciousness that always seemed to inflate him vanished—but only for a moment. For in the next moment, he mounted an ottoman and thrust all his zest into his performance. "Welcome to the Latrun Monastery, a hidden gem of history and tranquility in Israel. Built in 1927 by talented French Trappist Monks, this captivating haven holds immense historical significance, having once served as a formidable fortress during the British Mandate period." With each sentence, Hal's immense passion and opulent zeal permeated the room more and more and in such a way that all the guests began to feel as though they were floating through a palpable energy on the buoyancy of his phrases. "Today, the serene aura of Latrun Monastery captivates visitors as they explore the sacred enclave of the Order of Cistercians of the Strict Observance, renowned for their devotion to silence. The vast and mesmerizingly landscaped grounds welcome all, offering a soothing and peaceful refuge. The enchanting garden boasts a wondrous collection of late Classical and early Christian capitals and reliefs, each delicately crafted to tell stories of the past. Stepping into this artistic wonderland transports visitors to an era of brilliance and spiritual wonder." Hal took a deep breath. The speech was done.

"It sounds lovely, Hal." Gwen's face flushed. "You'll have to go, George."

"But what is it like?" George asked, cocking his neck out in waiting.

"What do you mean 'what is it like?'" replied Tom Clark, staring blankly at George. "Were you not listening to Hal's explanation?" Everyone but George laughed at this.

"I was listening. He told me about Latrun. He didn't tell me about his experience there. How it impacted him or what about the monastery he admired most."

"Georgie is right," conceded Hal. "I'd have to say what I admired most was the beautiful gardens and as for how it impacted me, well I'd say that it definitely made me think a lot about how something that was built to praise God and light can be used instead for the atrocities of war."

George did not look satisfied. "Tell me about the garden, Hal. Tell me about the flowers. What kind of flowers do they have there?"

The blithe presence that had pervaded every inch of the room during Hal's speech was now gone. Hal looked at George. "They got all sorts of lovely flowers in the garden th—"

"I know they must have all sorts, but I want to know exactly what sort to expect when I go there next month."

Hal smiled at George. It wasn't his most impressive smile, but it was still better than what most people could produce. "There's—"

"I think your original description was perfect, Hal," Gwen interrupted. "It even convinced George to do some sightseeing in Jerusalem next month. Anyway, I just got a text from the boys and there seems to be an issue in our basement with some flooding, so unfortunately, we will have to be leaving early. Sorry, Hal."

"No problem at all." Hal swooped down from the ottoman and gave Gwen a warm hug. He turned to George and offered a swift and firm hand. "Put'er there, George. I'm excited to hear about your trip to Latrun."

George and Gwen made their way upstairs and out the front door.

"You made a perfect ass of yourself in there. Why can't you just hang out and have a good time?"

"He's lying, Gwen. Anyway, that's not what's important. What's happening in the basement?"

Gwen stopped, laughing luridly. "I made that up, George, to get out of there so you'd stop embarrassing us. Are you that oblivious to how stupid you looked in there?"

"He's lying, Gwen. He's never been to Latrun. I'll bet he's never left Missouri! You can't just lie to all these people in order to get them to like you. It's wrong. It's strange, and it's wrong."

"We all like Hal. He's kind and generous." With that, Gwen walked ahead briskly, making her way to their home and leaving George alone on Hal Cox's front porch.

***

Sunday was typically the day that George had to himself when traveling for Rowles. His usual routine consisted of walking through the city near his hotel, checking reviews for the best places to eat, eating, and looking through stores for something that might interest Gwen, Alex, or Andrew. It wasn't vacationing to George. It was killing time. Although, George would never deny that he had been introduced to some pretty delicious food over the years. The food, like salve in a minor wound, made time away from home tolerable.

As George spooned down his Shakshuka in a cafe a block away from his hotel, he scrolled through reviews of restaurants, planning the rest of his meals for the day. He preferred to stay as near to his hotel as possible. Taking a taxi was too expensive, and just the thought of using public transit in a busy city produced stress in George. Of course, George had occasionally made a pilgrimage far from his hotel for eateries that were widely acclaimed or recommended by a friend. Widening his search parameters revealed a perfect five-star falafel joint. Usually, when a place had five stars, it was a fluke due to the fact that it had only one or two reviews.

Herzl's Falafel, however, remained at five stars after 1,742 reviews. George was nearly positive he would make it 1,743 after his visit. It was quite a bit out of the way, but if he left for that part of town right after breakfast then he'd make it there no problem.

As his eyes scanned the map for any places that might be worth visiting near the restaurant, he locked onto a spot less than 5 kilometers from Herzl's: Latrun.

***

Gwen had not been too happy with him after Hal's game night—and that was putting it nicely. She avoided talking to him for two days.

George's first night of silent treatment was spent watching *2001: A Space Odyssey* alone. The building dissonance of *Ligeti: Requiem: II Kyrie* matched and even seemed to enhance George's frustration with Hal. Yet, while Dr. Floyd and all his companions were disturbed by the obelisk, George was the only one vexed by Hal. Then came Hal 9000. This was George's favorite part of the film. As he observed Dave's attempt to outsmart the A.I., he was reminded of his own Hal.

It was sickening to watch a man who was clearly a fraud be so easily embraced by his neighbors and even his wife. In fact, they all seemed to prefer Hal over himself, and this was the thing that perturbed George Milton most. Everyone loved the lie of Hal Cox because they believed it—he wasn't a lie to them. But George could not unthink what he knew deep down.

The day after Hal's party, George decided that the best thing he could do was to remove Hal from his life and let things go back to normal. That proved to be near impossible. In a few weeks' time, Hal had become the nucleus of the neighborhood. He hosted small get-togethers weekly. He brought baked goods to people's front door regularly because "he had made too darn much of the things." He organized a cornhole league that met each Wednesday in his backyard. There was no escaping Hal.

George was relieved the day before his trip to Jerusalem, and for the first time ever he was excited to get away from home. He and Gwen were talking again, and she was ecstatic that George had agreed to visit Latrun. His trip to the monastery that Hal had so theatrically described was meant to be a peace offering. It would make Gwen happy. It would appease Hal. It would make everything square.

Though he had meant to keep the promise of visiting Latrun, he had completely forgotten until seeing it on the map. The fact that he was so busy with his trip that he had forgotten Hal for a bit made George smile. Yet, now that he remembered, he intended to keep his promise. The distance offered by the Atlantic provided some perspective, and George now saw that the episode at Hal's game night was his own fault. He had overreacted. Hal was a nice enough guy, and George now accepted that he would have to endure Hal's presence to keep his wife happy. It seemed a heavy price, but Gwen was worth every bit of it and more. And who knows, maybe Hal actually had visited all those places. A single guy with no kids. If he invested right and saved carefully, it was possible.

***

George had no idea how long he would need at Latrun, so he decided to do a little research. Most websites suggested an hour or two. As his inquiry continued, he came across a search result titled "Becky's Middle East Travel Blog | 10 Best Sites to See in Jerusalem." Gwen was always encouraging him to see more on his trips and, in hopes of gaining better graces with Gwen, he decided to give it a look. At number two, the list had "The Wailing Wall and the Jewish Quarter." Immediately, George imagined Tevye and his longing for time to read the Holy Book and to have a seat at the Eastern Wall. Lower down, George saw the "Garden Tomb," said to be the resting place of Christ before his resurrection. At number ten was Hal's Latrun. George read the caption below the image:

Welcome to the Latrun Monastery, a hidden gem of history and tranquility in Israel. Built in 1927 by talented French Trappist Monks, this captivating haven holds immense historical significance, having once served as a formidable fortress…

"Liar," George breathed aloud, a self-satisfied grin pulling itself up slowly. *It's all right here,* he thought. *Why would he memorize a caption from some travel blog? I know why. Because he's never been to Latrun, Rome, Sydney, or Cancun.*

George opened a new tab with his email and started typing a message to Gwen, but he stopped. Instead, he made immediate arrangements for a taxi to take him to the front gate of the Latrun Monastery.

The first cab agency he spoke with gave him an estimate of 200 Shekels one-way. George said that was perfect, and ten minutes later he was in the back seat on his way to the monastery.

He smiled the whole way there.

***

Two days after his return flight, Gwen sent George to the grocery store to get cooking wine. She had forgotten they were out and needed some for the roasted pork loin. George did not mind making trips to the grocery store. Shnucks was close, and its bakery always had samples of pastries sliced up in small slivers.

As George made his way to the bakery section, he spotted Hal. George's heart sank and then quickly rose to a hot, proud throbbing. With wide strides and heaving breaths, George Milton walked toward him. Hal Cox was holding two different hair growth treatments, seemingly deciding which one to buy. George did not notice this. His eyes were transfixed to Hal's profile. Without Hal's perceiving it, George arrived at his side.

"Hello, Hal," George said with polite indifference.

Hal started slightly and dropped the box of Miracle Hair Elixir. "Georgie! Mary, Joseph, and Moses, you got me good there, pal!" Hal said, as he attempted to discreetly hide the dropped product with one foot while hiding the other one behind his back. George noticed none of this as well. He had not blinked since he saw Hal. "What brings you to—"

"I got back from Jerusalem two days ago, Hal."

Hal smiled a big fat one. "That's right. You did, didn't you. How was—"

"I saw Latrun." George was smiling now. "I spent four hours there. I examined just about every inch of that old monastery."

"Ain't it beautiful, Georgie? Ah, I'd love to go back someday," Hal said and smiled wistfully as he shook his head and looked off somewhere in the distance toward where he thought Latrun must be.

"I bet you would, Hal. I gotta say, though, while the flowers were very beautiful like you said, my favorite thing on the whole grounds was the stained-glass depicting Thomas when he saw the resurrected Christ. It was so carefully crafted and the colors seemed vibrant like a high-resolution HD display. What did you think of that stained glass?"

Hal nodded with awe etched in every line and feature of his face. "Oh yeah, the stained window with Saint Tommy truly is a wonder."

"And what about that massive statue in the garden of David slaying Goliath? I mean, talk about breathtaking."

Hal continued to nod, "Ab-sow-lootly, that was one of the highlights of my visit as well."

George paused for a moment. He stared at Hal.

Hal hated silence. He began to strike up some banter, but George interrupted him.

"Hal, I made that stuff up. Everything I just said? Made up. I explored the grounds of Latrun like a CSI. I looked at every artifact. I smelled every scent. I touched the walls. I felt the rough ridges of the palm trees. I even spoke with the groundskeepers. I took in everything that Latrun had to offer, and the stained glass of Thomas and the statue of David were not part of it. They don't exist."

"What do you mean? I, uh. I mean, why would you make those things up, George?" Hal's worried confusion grew with each word.

"I know you lied about all your trips. I know that your description of Latrun was a recitation of a web page. I know that your family burger recipe consists of a ten-minute drive to Dempsey's." George Milton stopped and waited for Hal's response.

Nothing came. Hal's head simply drooped down until it could sink no lower, his shoulders following suit. He stared at the ground for what felt like a pocket eternity to George.

In what was to be his moment of triumph, George felt sick, the kind of sick he felt when his stomach was empty or when his pants were too tight. George began again, "And the worst part of these lies, Hal, is that they are unnecessary. My wife, the whole cul-de-sac, they all love ya. Hell, I can't blame them. You truly are one of the most generous, energetic, and friendly people I have ever met. You are a bit much for me, but I can't deny the appeal. They would have loved you just the same without all this world traveler business. I can't wrap my head around why—"

"Thank you, George. I think I'm gonna head home now," Hal interrupted. He reached down, picked up the box of Miracle Elixir, returned it to the shelf, and then let the hand behind his back fall to his side. George watched as Hal walked to the cash register, paid for whatever was in the other box, and left the store. His exit was slow and clumsy, his steps like the final *pffts* of air out of a loose balloon.

George felt guilt for a moment, the sort of guilt a child feels when they're caught stealing something. He stood thinking a while. When his web of thoughts led him to Gwen, he remembered the cooking wine and began to walk. Bottle in hand, George checked out and left the store without tasting his free pastry sample.

***

Nobody ever saw Hal after that night. Gwen called him a few days later to invite him over, but he briefly said he was going out of town to visit a sick relative and that he was unable to make it.

The week after that, there was a for sale sign in his front yard.

A month later they had new neighbors, a small elderly couple that could have been typecast in practically any film set in suburban America.

The husband wore sweater vests, used a four-pronged cane, and seemed to hate everything except his wife—and even her he seemed only to endure. The wife was the perfect thickness of classic grandma, with white curly hair cut short, and a disposition that was only outbrighted by the stars on a clear night.

The week after they moved in, Gwen invited them over for dinner. The husband loudly informed the table that the food was too spicy and that he intended to get McDonalds afterwards. The wife said to ignore him because he was an ornery grouch and that the dinner was lovely. She asked for the recipe and wrote it in her small leather-bound stationary as Gwen read it to her. She called everyone dear and over the course of the evening managed to compliment every object in the dining room.

Once dinner was over, they ate dessert on the back porch. As they spooned down their bowls of ice cream, the wife began to speak. "I noticed a considerably large film collection on our way outside. Who here is the cinephile?"

"That would be me," said George with a smile.

"They do make amazing films these days with all of the computer effects that are possible," the wife said. "Myself, I prefer the classics. *Sunset Boulevard. Gone with the Wind.* They didn't need a computer to be special. It was all in the writing, directing, and acting."

"I couldn't agree more," chimed George, "though I do like a good fun summer blockbuster."

"Meh," snarled the husband. "Movies are a *waste.* My father gave me a nickel to see a picture some afternoons when I was a boy. But I wouldn't go. I'd tell him I'd see a picture, but I wouldn't go. I saved all those nickels and when I was sixteen years old, those nickels covered the down payment on my Buick. You think I'd have had a car at that age if I wasted my money on pictures?"

"Probably not," said the wife, "but you might be a little more fun and pleasant than you are now, Henry."

"Movies are all fantasy. Fantasy never did anything good for anybody. How can it? It's not real," the husband said.

"Well, we cinephiles, as your wife put it, know that the movies aren't real," said George jovially. "We know that it's all actors and sets, but it doesn't matter because the emotion and the essence of the human experience that is explored in a good film *is* real."

"Phooey," said the husband with a nod. Alex and Andrew laughed at this. Gwen and the wife couldn't help but chuckle themselves.

The night ended with a goodbye at the door and the promise of another dinner sometime soon, but it never happened. Gwen didn't seem to mind that it never happened, and George absolutely didn't mind. The old couple were the best sort of neighbors. They kept their yard in good shape, they kept streetside conversations concise, and they were mostly aloof.

SANDRA MCCOMPUTER FACE

She was hot. *Awooga Awooga* hot. Green face Jim Carrey with jaw dropping to the table hot. So hot I took my AirPods out—well, one of my AirPods. The other played half of the stereo recording of Fleetwood Mac's "Gypsy." It sounded about the same. At least I couldn't tell anything was missing.

And I went over to this hottie. She had walked right past me in her short red spaghetti strap cocktail dress and was now seated legs crossed in the corner of the café. Her legs were thin and muscular, like the kind drawn on Jean Grey and Storm in those '90s *X-Men* comics. Hubba hubba. Her waist was perfect. I don't know measurements and sizes, but hot damn was that waist petite and tight. Until I saw her that day, I believed the hourglass figure was just something for cartoons and supermodels with eating disorders. Nope. This body on this woman was like Jessica Rabbit brought to life but without the overly big butt and honkers. Everything looked proportional.

And each proportion was a delight that I eyed hot-heartedly as I walked up to her.

My rising gaze met her face—er well, her screen.

Resting on her neck was an all-in-one computer monitor, a tannish gray model from the early 2000s. It was open to the desktop of the operating system. The desktop wallpaper was a still shot of Meg Ryan in a red wig holding a colorful sign that read "Joseph Banks."

"Hiya," I purred with a wink. "*Joe Versus the Volcano* is a great movie. Meg Ryan really nailed all those roles."

The computer screen remained unchanged, and her body did not budge.

"My—uh—dad, he loved that movie. We used to watch it all the time. 'Looks like we're in for a blow.'" I leaned in closer now. Her scent was intoxicating, like all the best smells from the perfume section of a department store. Her skin looked so milky and unblemished as though it had never been touched, not even by her. In my peripheral, I saw her monitor flash. When I looked up at the monitor, Meg Ryan had been replaced by a blank white wallpaper.

I wet my lips. I was hot all over. I needed this woman to love me.

"I'm Porter," I said. And then I grinned as I leaned in further.

A Word document opened on the screen. She typed out a message. Here is what it said:

I am Sandra McComputer Face. Please leave me alone.

I stroked the top of the monitor. "You don't even know me. Let's go out to dinner sometime. Let's say this weekend. Are you free this weekend?"

NO NO

NO NO

The *NOs* covered the entire computer screen. And yet, when I put my hand tenderly on her shoulder, there was no recoil. The skin was so soft and so warm and so welcoming. Something must have been malfunctioning in the computer.

So, I called the Geek Squad at Best Buy and they told me to bring her over. When I grabbed her hand, she stood up and came along with me. Yet more and more *NOs* typed themselves out frantically, and I could hear a faint whirring sound from the monitor. Then there was a smell like overheated plastic and metal.

They sure have gotten a lot better at making computers that work and don't overheat nowadays. This thing on her shoulders really was an outdated piece of junk.

***

After tinkering with the monitor for twenty minutes or so, the Geek Squad guy said that the computer was so old that there was nothing he could do. I pointed with a thumb to the now headless paragon standing next to me, and I asked him if I could buy a new computer for her head. He told me the only model that would work ran $3,000.

"No head at all ain't so bad," I said to the Geek Squad guy.

"No it's not," he said, and he stroked his chin as he eyed the headless body.

***

I left the all-in-one computer in the trunk and walked her into my apartment. I laid her down on the couch. I laid down on top of her. I kissed her neck. Her hand stroked my hair. I let my hands wander, wander, wander. I was all fire and sweat and electricity. The feeling I felt when I first saw her returned. I quaked. She quaked too. We were both warm and caught in the throes of intimacy. Then I reached lower. I reached—

There was nothing. It was like a Barbie Doll down there, slick and hard like a fiberglass fender. I jumped from the sofa. Her arms reached out to me. I looked away in disgust.

After pacing the room for a few minutes, I pushed her toward the front door. I herded her into the car. I drove to the café where we'd met only hours before. I put the monitor back on her head, straightened her dress out, and pushed her toward the café.

As she walked through the door, heads turned and jaws dropped.

She was hot. *Awooga Awooga* hot.

I put my other airpod back in and tried to remember how it felt when I thought she was real.

DEVIL'S PUNCHBOWL

Reed Fallow was bored. Everyone was bored. Boredom was a game that everyone played and that everyone won, and everyone was perfectly miserable for it. This is how the game worked.

People in those days had everything at their fingertips. A slick little luminous brick reflected in their eyes, and in its light were coded and pixelated copies of everything that existed in the material world. The glowing box could show the definition of any word (like *fallow* for instance), or images of any street in Paris, or every word of political discourse spoken at the United States capitol, or the 1988 film *Earth Girls are Easy*, or any episode of the *Super Friends* cartoon, or the lyrics to "Roll With The Punches" by Young MC; however, it was mostly used to show women who made careers of making sex look fulfilling and enjoyable no matter how demeaning and depraved their male counterparts acted (making things pretty awful for women in the material world—as if it wasn't bad enough for them there already).

The way the boredom game worked was that people would stare at the glowing brick for hours, and—being able to see everything—they would look at the stuff that amused them most until it did not amuse them any longer and that was when the boredom game was won. Then they would pick a new thing that amused them and make the box show it to them, and shortly after, another round of the game would be complete.

On that day, Reed Fallow had won the boredom game 212 times. It was 8:17 AM. It had been a slow morning, and he was nowhere near his usual victory count. He pressed a button on the light box. The box went dark.

As its glow disappeared, the room that he must have been in for the last few hours appeared around him. It was flooded with natural light pouring in from three large windows along the wall in front of him. Yet this solar luminescence seemed dim when compared to the light from the box, and the room (though decorated with various objects of unique hues) looked muted and dead to Reed.

Each image that materialized on the light box was clearly defined in vibrant colors that the light box companies claimed were the most accurate depictions possible of those colors. A Granny Smith on a light box screen was a transcendent green that flooded your eyes with a verdance like that of a thousand grassy fields compressed into a flaring lightning bolt; and so when you picked up a Granny Smith at the supermarket, it resembled a sickly frail version of the apple on the light box.

And so it was with the room that Reed found himself in. The hues of the hotel bed sheets seemed less like the red of crimson lipstick and more like the tongue of a dead dog flopped out across the mattress. The navy walls stood there like the understudy to the understudy of the fathomed navy that the lightbox had shown to Reed just moments before. Worse still was the blue of the ocean that lay past the window, crashing in frothy grayed tones across a sandy gray shore. Reality muted everything.

No clouds. Not even a strand of jet exhaust marred the clear sky above the coast. Reed went to the window and observed the sea. *Why do they call it the big blue*? he thought. *It isn't blue at all.* And it wasn't. The flame-kissed disc in the sky cast all of its light on that expanse of water, and it was still gray and so was the shoreline that the waves threw themselves upon. Dead tones. Hues that belonged in a color wheel mausoleum, remnants of the spectrum that constituted all of reality before the light boxes.

Reed looked down at his box once more. It lit up for him as he stared at it, revealing a picture of Reed with his arm around a woman who appeared close to him in age (which was 29 currently but the picture was eight years old), the time of day (which was now 8:22 AM), the date (which was December 28th, 2027), and the current weather in Lincoln City, OR (which was 49 degrees Fahrenheit, clear skies, and winds at 22 miles per hour). He clicked the light box off and was once again in the room.

When people were bored, really bored, they convinced themselves that they needed to "get out." Nobody knew what this meant. It did not mean getting out of the building that they were in because simply stepping outside would not accomplish what "getting out" was meant to accomplish. To the best of my knowledge and the knowledge of everyone else who lived in that time, "getting out" was less of an action and more of a shift in mental state. Once out, an individual was somehow removed from their normal routine, and this disruption to the standard operating procedure was supposed to produce a heightened emotional, spiritual, sexual, physical, or mental state by introducing disruption. People often "went out" to a place that looked remarkably similar to the place they had just "gotten out" of. But it was not the same, and so it was "out."

Reed Fallow was very bored and so he decided that the time had come to get out. The light box showed him things to do nearby. One of the things it showed him was the Devil's Punchbowl. The coastal rock formation was 16.5 miles away from Reed's hotel.

***

Reed Fallow drove his 2005 Toyota Camry down the Oregon Coastal Highway. The main drag of Lincoln City was just that. The walls of the buildings must have been bright with fresh paint at some point in the past and must have drawn tourists to their doors and along their sidewalks. Reed could tell that the candy store he passed was once red like a glossy candy apple. No longer. The paint had faded to something between a lightly syrupped cherry snow cone and a hunk of sushi-grade salmon that had seen a ghost. A sign hung in the window flipped to the "open" side, but the lights appeared to be off and the store looked empty. Apollo himself could not have conjured a sunnier day, but even unfiltered celestial rays could not make the buildings or their chipping paint sparkle. Not a soul strolled along the strip besides the occasional teen cultist with a hoodie slung up over their head. He'd seen about ten of them so far, all in black hoodies with the strings pulled tight to conceal most of their faces.

Cultist teens. The term was redundant given that nearly all cultists were teens and almost all teens were cultists. Reed had been in a cult until his first year at Granger State: the Slender Digit Granfallooners. It was a meme cult. They all were. Designed by teens to mock the organized religion of their parents and other adults. Their rules, their creeds, their rites, and their rituals all founded upon pop culture, absurdist humor, and a general indifference to anything "sacred."

The Slender Digit Granfallooners only accepted individuals whose ring size was an 8 or below. The central figure of their devotion was FrazPitz69, an absurdist content creator who died at the age of 17 from blood loss. He lost all of his blood because his left arm was ripped off while recording a video about making lemonade using a wood chipper. A true entertainer, Frazpitz69 was hopped up on wizzies at the time and told the cameraman to continue filming as he used his remaining arm to drink a glass of lemonade, blood and marrow mixed in. Then he fell dead.

Eugene Wertz, FrazPitz69's reality identity, was given a traditional funeral service by his parents who, like the rest of the world, were entirely unaware of his digital persona. It wasn't until the lemonade video was posted online four years later by the cameraman that Frazpitz69 became an overnight icon.

Adults saw Frazpitz69 as everything wrong with youth. Young people saw Frazpitz69 as a direct contradiction of all the stupid things adults valued immensely. Soon after, a 15-year-old in Indianapolis inspired by FrazPits69 and Vonnegut's *Cat's Cradle* founded the Slender Digit Granfallooners with FrazPits69 as its figurehead. It was the first meme cult. Their main ritual entailed dealing a good old-fashioned smash to the digits of any "fat fingers" dumb enough to leave their hands exposed flat on a surface. With their cult-issued FrazBar, they'd smack the wooden pipe down with the careless force of Samson, crushing their victim's fingers and shouting "for the Fraz!"

As with any cult, some followers lived out their faith in manic devotion while others were simply along for the ride. Reed was the latter. Joining a cult was necessary in the teen years for protection and a sense of belonging. He chose the Slender Digit Granfallooners for the reason most teens joined their cults: Reed had a crush on one of its members.

Fay Geene Weathersby was lovely in all the best contradictory ways. She had a small face but a pronounced nose that was as sharp as her deadpan wit. Her eyes were empty but filled to the brim with wild green fire that danced as she stared languidly at the world around. Her thick strawberry locks hung down past her shoulders, but she always kept them up and hidden behind a bandana. She was tall, but you would never have known it as she spent most of her life slouched in a chair, sprawled on the ground, or curled in a bed.

Once, on a snowy January day, Reed watched as Fay stood up, removed her bandana and all her clothes, and walked slowly out into the field that lay below the hill the two sat upon. She walked twenty feet out into icy white expanse, fell forward on her face, and proceeded to make a snow angel as her bare white bottom jiggled softly with each swift motion.

Reed said nothing. He even looked away after he perceived that Fay was disrobing. He felt unworthy, and he secretly believed that this was some test, that a normal man, a lesser man, would have looked. That she would see that he, a great man, did not look. But she never looked back, and even if she had, Reed would not have seen. His eyes looked back to the city of Franklin, Missouri, the many steeples of its many churches poking up here and there above the treetops.

From that day forward Reed believed that he was destined for greatness, and that greatness was to marry Fay Geene Weathersby, bed her in reverence, and spend the rest of his life thanking FrazPitz69 or God or whoever for giving him the one thing that could make him happiest: the love of a person you do not deserve.

***

Reed Fallow continued south on the coastal highway. He was out of Lincoln City now and the road was winding to stay parallel to the bay. Bay. That made him think of the woman in the picture on the light box. Her name was *not* Bay. Her name *was* Fay. Fay Geene Weathersby. Fay was supposed to meet him in Lincoln City sometime in the next few days. That was all she had texted him.

Meet me in Lincoln City, OR. I'll be there in a few days.

He texted "okay," packed his bags, and left his apartment in St. Louis 33 minutes later.

***

"It's all so stupid, fake, and pointless," Fay had told Reed one night in the Dairy Queen parking lot, "and that's why I *love* it."

Fay was first to volunteer at any cult event from new inductee finger measuring to building FrazShrines around town. When Fay smashed fingers with her little baton, she carefully put all her weight and force into each blow. The victims would be in such shock from the attack that they would just stare at their throbbing fingers. By the time they looked up, Fay was gone. At prayer meetings, Fay made all the lemonade, carefully adding just the right amount of manufactured theatrical blood to the drink. She cried the loudest during the prayers, her left arm FrazShaking so violently that it looked like a snake that just bit into an electrical cord. But it was all a stupid act. Everything was stupid, and so by committing so completely to the stupidest thing of all, Fay felt power. More than felt it, she radiated with it. A glowing and humming exuberance permeated every space she stepped into.

Reed Fallow applied to Granger State only because he knew it was Fay's dream school. There was a professor there, Dr. Phineas T. Furantur, whose research focused on the study of meme cults. Fay wanted to peel back the curtain, to ascertain the true values and impacts of meme cults. While most adolescents' interest in their cult waned during the senior year of high school,

Fay's was greater than ever. She was even unable to attend graduation because she'd smashed some "fat fingers" so hard that she fractured the woman's index finger. That did not stop the woman from pointing her out in a police line-up, landing Fay two nights behind bars.

Fay's grades were excellent, and her entrance essay keenly explained her desire to work with Dr. Furantur. She was accepted with a scholarship. It turns out the admissions committee at Granger saw her incarceration as evidence of everything Fay expressed in her essay. An immense intellect who had unparalleled knowledge of and commitment to the world's oldest meme cult, who better than Fay Geene Weathersby to work with Dr. Furantur?

Reed Fallows got into Granger for one reason and one reason only: his admissions essay. His intellect was average. His grades were average. His test scores were average. But his determination to follow Fay was matched only by Napoleon's desire to conquer. It was this determination that enabled Reed to produce one of the most beautiful and bogus admissions letters ever written. It told of his awful and underprivileged childhood spent in poverty (Reed's parents were the kindest people and his father's actuary salary provided quite a comfortable life), his struggling on tests no matter how many hours he spent studying (Reed did not study for a single test his entire high school career), and of course the death of his sister Bethany—whose dream it was to attend Granger—during his senior year (Reed was an only child).

During their first year at college, Reed and Fay hung out most weekends. They spent most of those weekends staking out the haunts of the local Slender Digit Granfallooners and other meme cults. Fay would study them, taking meticulous notes. She would talk to Reed about the untapped power of meme cults, how meme cults could be the embryonic stage of a great social movement, a movement that could legitimize teenagers and enable youths across the world to work collectively to solve this generation's most trying problems.

Reed would listen. He would watch her lips move and inhale deeply, drinking Fay's natural fragrance. Her intoxicating effervescence would rattle his lungs and make his fingers quake like an old car idling.

In her sophomore year, Fay got a research assistantship with Dr. Furantur, a position usually reserved for graduate students. Reed would see her once a month if he was lucky, and it was always a rushed conversation when they ran into each other on campus. Fay would be distant, asking the same questions every time: "How have you been? What classes are you taking?"

A normal man would have taken the hint that Fay's life was moving forward and that he, Reed, was not a part of it. But Reed was not a normal man. He saw this as another test. He did not get bothered by the obvious decline of their relationship. He had faith, and this faith was founded on a simple principle: nobody loved Fay more than he did and nobody could possibly be a better friend, partner, and spouse to her than he could.

Their junior year his faith was rewarded. One night, Fay showed up at his apartment at half past midnight. Her eyes were red and puffy, her nose stuffed, and her rain-soaked hair hung down from her bandanaless head. She immediately hugged Reed, a physical interaction the two had never shared. She kissed

Reed. Reed kissed her. They held each other on his couch for hours before she finally spoke.

"You never truly believed any of it, right? The Granfallooners?" she asked in the darkness.

"No."

"I knew you didn't. I guessed it, but you were so quiet and so observant. I don't know why I never asked back then." When she spoke, her voice flooded the darkness, her words filling the room, shaping the room, becoming the room.

"You would always tell me that you didn't believe any of it," Reed said. "But I never wanted to say the real reason that I appeared to be so devout."

"And why was that?" Her voice revealed a smile that the darkness failed to conceal.

"I was in love with you. I am in love with you. You are the reason I was a Granfallooner, the reason I came to Granger."

Fay pulled Reed's head down and kissed him again. The fire of years of anticipation consumed his body once more as they kissed. *Faith rewarded*, Reed thought. They held each other until morning came. Then Fay got up, walked out the door, and did not make any attempt to communicate with Reed until six years later when she sent a text.

Meet me in Lincoln City, OR. I'll be there in a few days.

***

The day was overcast now. Reed sat in his parked car. Dozens of cultist teens congregated at the lookout point, all in black hoodies, staring down at what must have been the Devil's Punchbowl.

Reed was unsure what the Punchbowl actually was. He pulled out his light box and found what looked like the attraction's official website. It showed a red rock formation shaped like a sort of coliseum that looked to be the size of a football field. The walls of the formation had some openings that brought in foamy tides that would periodically fill the Punchbowl. The website featured only one image: a wide shot of the coastal landmark filled with swarms of people who appeared to be swimming. The caption read, "give yourself to the water and find yourself in the punch." Reed looked up from the light box and once more at the cultists. Their arms were now raised. They swayed forward and backward. Reed got out of the car.

As Reed walked toward the hooded crowd, a tow truck passed. Resting on the back of the tow truck was a gray compact SUV. It had Missouri plates and the back window had a Granger State decal in the bottom left corner. Reed pulled out his light box and phoned Fay. It went straight to voicemail.

Reed pushed his way through the mass of swaying teens to the lookout point. They were singing along to a song that played on all their light boxes. The song was "Roll with the Punches" by Young MC.

As Reed continued to make his way through, teens took notice of him. Nudges rippled through the crowd as pointed fingers and hushes cast a spotlight on the outsider. Soon people began to grab Reed and thrust him forward. Once at the front of the throng, he was thrown to the ground. Reed raised his head.

The figure before him untied its hoodie strings and let the hood fall, revealing the face of a beautiful young woman. Her skin was a dusky olive, the coastal wind flapped her jet-black hair in chaotic spasms, and her fierce gray eyes lasered down upon Reed with volcanic disdain. She raised both her hands high. The music and the singing stopped.

"What is this thing before me?" she asked the silent crowd.

"An ingredient!" they screamed back in unison.

"That's right. And why does the great FrazPitz69 give us ingredients?" She asked, louder now.

"To make the true drink, the true blood punch!"

"And who makes the true punch? Do you?" She gestured to the cultists with both arms.

"No! The Fraz makes the true punch in his punchbowl!"

Reed began to address the young woman, but he was kicked silent by several cultists.

"You don't speak, ingredient," said the young woman. "You are a thing, and things don't speak. Things don't act. Things are acted upon." She gave a backhanded swat to the air in front of her, and four cultists grabbed Reed by each of his limbs and carried him off toward the Punchbowl.

Reed pleaded and sobbed as they carried him. "I was a Granfallooner. I—I—I was one of you. You—" a blow to the head cut him short.

"We are not a part of the Slender Digit Granfallooners, ingredient. And even if we were, it would mean nothing. The Granfallooners are the creation of some friendless sex-depraved pubescent nerd holed up in his bedroom. They are an affront to the Fraz. But Arabella communes with the Fraz. She knows his will."

"It's all a meme. This whole—" another blow to the head.

"Adults all say the same things. But be happy, ingredient. You will be a part of the great beverage. One day, when we have gathered enough ingredients, Frazpits69 himself will return. He will drink the true drink that he once tried to brew himself. His arm will grow back stronger, and with that arm, he will heal and rule this broken world."

They were on the beach now. The arched entryway to the Punchbowl lay before them. It was low tide. Hundreds of bodies lay sprawled out among the boulders and sand within the stadiumesque rock formation.

Reed's captors swung him back and forth, building momentum and eventually letting go. The flat face of a boulder met Reed's nose. The boulder did not move. Reed's nose cracked, then it throbbed, and then it began to ooze blood like a half-closed faucet. Trying to stop the bleeding with one hand, Reed stood and began to walk back to the archway.

The four cultists turned and saw Reed attempting to escape. One of them, a tall figure with a body like an armored tank, walked back toward Reed. Punch after punch, kick after kick, the tank beat all the resistance and all the strength out of Reed.

"Hurry up, Tito. The tide's rolling in," one of the other figures yelled across the Punchbowl.

Tito the Tank dealt one more fisted blow to Reed's stomach, let Reed's limp body fall to the ground, and then returned to his group. Reed did not watch them walk away. He looked at the sky, gasping and moaning.

Water began to touch his feet periodically. Then it began to cover his legs. Soon the tide tossed Reed's weary body to and fro within the Punchbowl. The tide was rhythmic and consistent. Occasionally Reed would bump into another body. It was hard to tell if they were alive or not—nobody seemed to make sound or perhaps the crashing waves drowned out any sounds they attempted. Reed may have been screaming, but there was no way to tell. He lay on his back, floating like a punctured raft, his body congruent and seemingly glued to the surface of the ever-shifting water.

Reed looked up. The red rock of the surrounding formation stood out to him all at once. Reed could not remember ever having seen such a vibrant hue of red. It was the red of blood on white linoleum, the red of fresh meat in the jaws of a lion, the red of the witch's poison apple, the red of Mars and all of its mountains, the red of a thousand times a thousand crimson balloons eclipsing the sky and sun and yet refracting all the solar rays of that star they concealed. Reed felt peace. Reed felt that he was truly connected to something for the first time in his life, something larger than reality.

The tide was higher now. The foamy waves carried and tossed all the inhabitants of the Punchbowl. Reed gasped for air each time his head broke the surface. But he felt no fear. The tide receded, leaving a rock beached Reed half alive and yet more alive than he had ever been.

Reed wished to speak to Fay, to share this with her. He pulled out his light box. The screen was cracked, but the device appeared to be functional.

"Call Fay," he whispered to the light box. It was a hoarse but peaceful whisper.

"Calling Fay," the light box responded. The lightbox spoke matter-of-factly. It did not seem to understand the reality of the situation.

There was a ring. Then there was another sound nearby, a jingling ringtone coming from some other lightbox. Reed sat up and surveyed his surroundings, searching for the source of the ringtone. Laying in a sobbing heap ten feet from his rock was Fay Geene Weathersby. Her body was bruised and bloodied, and yet her beauty remained untouched. Reed crawled to her and laid down beside her.

"You came, Reed," she managed to say between her heaved sobs. Her voice was weak but sincere.

"Of course."

"Do you remember the night I came to your apartment all those years ago?"

"Of course." Reed held her close now. He held her for a long time until she started to speak once more.

"That night—that night Dr. Furantur told me the true origin of meme cults. He told me that there never was any FrazPitz69. The video was a fake. Eugene Wertz never existed. The meme cults were made by corporations and government entities to instill a sense of meaning and purpose in teens, to get them to make harmless mischief on purpose, to subjugate them."

"Why should that matter?" Reed asked. "You believed all the cult stuff was fake anyway. Why should the nature of its fakeness matter?"

"Because," Fay's voice took on an accusatory tone, "it was supposed to be grassroots. It was supposed to be evidence of the creativity and ingenuity of the teenage mind, a testament to the demographic's potential…"

Fay croaked on in dense philosophical strands of thought, but Reed was not listening. The tide rolled back in and lifted the pair from the ground. Reed held Fay close as she cried and shook, gasping for air.

Reed was happy.

He had everything that he ever wanted.

Then a large rolling wave dashed the two against the wall of the Punchbowl, and Reed saw the most beautiful red branch out from him and into the water all around.

And then Reed saw everything.

And then he saw nothing.

THE LAST AMERICAN FACTORY FARM

Franklin Graves did not eat gym-slaughtered meat, and he was proud of the fact. So proud that he started a podcast about his refusal to eat gym-slaughtered meat and his refusal to violence animals. Nearly everyone knew of the podcast and of Graves as a figure. Almost nobody put any stock in what the podcast preached. The few people who did follow the podcast sincerely were very similar to Franklin Graves.

The persona of Franklin Graves was this: Graves was an eternal complainer who did nothing about the things he complained about beyond the act of complaining. He had made a career out of complaining. His podcast of complaints was ridiculed and trafficked so frequently that Graves was able to live somewhat comfortably off ad revenue. Somewhat comfortably meant that Graves had a one-room apartment, plenty of cruelty-free meat to eat, and a worn Lazy Boy which he used for leisure, labor, and rest.

Franklin Graves stood far from the crowd of tourists. The tourists all chittered and pointed up at the industrial building before them. Above the awning of the building's entrance sat a large sign written in bold red ink. The sign said this: "Welcome to the Last Automated Animal Slaughterhouse in America." Franklin Graves spat in disgust as he observed the tourists. He hated them. He hated almost everyone. He believed that almost everyone enjoyed evil. He believed that he was pulling back the curtain on that evil. He believed he was the last true journalist. He believed he could wake people up. That was the name of his podcast: Wake Up, People!

Graves's touring of the facility was in fact an attempt at waking people up. Like his podcast, it was an act of complaining—only with a captive physical audience. This was his second attempted tour. The first was an absolute failure. He had lost his composure and screamed wildly at the tour guide, the same tour guide who now emerged from the large double doors of the building.

The guide gave a small bow and gestured toward the doors with his arms. "Please follow me into the slaughterhouse antechamber. Unless, of course, you would all prefer to be beaten upon by this relentless heat?"

The tour group chuckled. There were around 60 of them shuffling steadily from the balmy Midwest summer blaze into the ice-laden arms of the air-conditioned building. Graves shuffled in last, pulling up the collar of his khaki trench coat in an attempt to conceal his round, greasy face.

While the antechamber barely accommodated the mass of guests, its 30-foot walls—complete with an ornate domed roof—gave the impression of being in a much larger room. The tourists scanned the walls, the paintings, the enlarged newspaper clippings, and the meticulous baroque trim work all done in glimmering gold. Were it not for the bizarre artwork and news snippets, one may have thought themselves in some corner of Versailles.

"If you please," began the guide, "direct your attention to this first framed news story from the *Jefferson Leader*." The guide wore a mauve fitted suit that clearly outlined his thin but muscular body. His aubergine tie sat stiffly behind his buttoned coat and against his perfectly ironed salmon dress shirt. Everything about the man was polished, from his shoes to his diction. A pristine painter's brush mustache of brown moved subtly as the guide spoke. "The story to which you now look was published by a small newspaper only five miles from this very edifice. The date of publication was December 5th, 2023. Could I secure a volunteer to read the headline for us?" He surveyed the group with eyebrows raised and lips pursed. A little ginger-haired girl with freckles and a tooth gap lunged her hand toward the domed ceiling. "Please, young lady, read on." The guide smiled softly, his attentive gaze resting on the girl as she read.

She read in slow deliberate syllables. "Jefferson War Hawks Defeat Willsboro 38-27 to Claim 4A State Football Title."

"Very well done, miss. You truly are a stupendous reader, aren't you? Isn't she, everyone?" The guide looked gleamingly to the crowd. He began to applaud, and the visitors followed. "Take a curtsy for your devotees, darling."

The little girl curtsied gently, her face taking on the hue of her hair as she flashed a clumsy smile.

"Now," began the guide, clapping his hands together, "why would I start the tour by drawing your attention to this little morsel of *ancient* news, hmm?"

A much larger and much hairier hand raised itself this time. "Because that's the team that started the insane cult that has our whole country bashing in the heads of defenseless animals with baseball bats."

The guide wore a rehearsed smile. "Mr. Graves, you must absolutely adore touring our facility. This is your second time this week. Ladies and gentlemen, may I introduce to you a man who needs no introduction, our friend Mr. Franklin Graves, a journalist for the—which publication was it again?"

A bald man who wore a tight white polo shirt and had the figure of a bodybuilder hollered, "Wake Up, People!" Scattered laughs broke out among the guests.

Graves looked at the man in the polo shirt. "Brand recognition," Graves shouted. "I must be doing something right." The crowd stepped back from Graves as much as they could in the limited space of the antechamber. They looked at him like he was the source of some malignant odor—which, thanks to his lack of hygiene, he was. A few even began to verbally harass Graves, but the guide cut them off. Still, they all glared at Graves, hatred resting on their lips and brows.

Franklin Graves was a larger man in every sense of the word. He stood at six foot seven inches. His gut hung out over his belt and swayed when he walked. His fleshy arms hung heavy with fat that pulled his stretched skin down toward the ground. Days' worth of patchy salt and pepper stubble resided on his face. In his hands, Graves carried a small notepad and a number

#2 pencil, a seeming parody of reporters before the digitization of the world—but Graves was in earnest. The pencil's tip, irregular and crooked, appeared to have been sharpened by a knife.

"Now," began the guide, "the purpose for our looking at this article—as Mr. Graves so charmingly elucidated—is to start our tour by establishing the history that led to this becoming the last automated animal slaughtering facility on the North American continent."

Franklin Graves let out a sigh of disgust as he looked around for similar reactions, but nobody shared his sentiment. Now that the guide was speaking, nobody seemed to even notice Graves.

"The 2023 Jefferson Missouri War Hawk Football team was the first team from Jefferson High School to win the 4A state championship. How did these youngsters, who only a season before lost every single game, manage to win the state title?" Once more the guide perused the visitors' raised hands. Just as he decided which hand to select, a gruff voice broke the silence.

"They won," Graves said in a phlegm crackled breath, "because they changed their workout regimen and—oh yeah—they also started a demented cult, the god of which they—" Graves was cut short by a violent coughing fit that ended with thick liquid flying from his mouth and splattering on the floor. "Excuse me," he said, covering the mucous with his untied boots. "The god of which they credit for their victory." His second attempt at this phrase was delivered mockingly with confidence. He clearly had hoped to get a chuckle or two from the other visitors, but they only stared at him, clear lines of annoyance drawn on their faces.

"Very close, my fellow. No, *they* did not start the cult. The cult *was* however created by a young man by the name of Kyson Jaxon Bauer, a high school sophomore at the time. As the story goes, Mr. Bauer beat a local farmer's sheep to death with a baseball bat after misinterpreting a poem in his English Class. The poem, "The Lamb" by Louis T. Trippet, can be seen here." The guide directed the guests to another spot on the wall where the poem rested in a massive frame. The poem went like this:

Blood, oh blood, that trickles over the eyes
and obscures the vision of the visionary.
Crimson paint made to beat in the heart
and pulse through the body
is now smeared on the pure white canvas
of the lamb.
They beat on the lamb.
They beat on the lamb.
They beat him blind and bloody.
Still, he sees forever.
His eyes do not rest in sockets.
His eyes rest in and on eternity.

After the guide read the poem, he asked if anyone in the group could interpret it. No hands went up this time. "The poem," began the guide, "is truly substandard and laborious. It is not in a single anthology or textbook nor has any other teacher in the history of the United States claimed to have ever taught it. Only Mrs. Bellingham of Jefferson, Missouri and only that year, her final year before retirement, did she teach the poem.

Louis T. Trippett only published three poems in total, the others just as contrived and soaked in overt Christian symbolism. At that time, all three poems could be found only on Christianpoetryforum.com. The theory is that Mrs. Bellingham selected the poem on a whim after reading it on the forum which records indicate she frequented.

"Regardless of why she read the poem to her classes that day, the choice would lead Kyson Jaxon Bauer to bludgeon a defenseless little sheep to death. That bludgeoning would echo through the history of this nation and be the first ripple in a wave that has ushered in an era of unparalleled health and safety in the United States of America."

"Health and safety for people, but what about the animals? What about the cows at slaughter gyms across the country?" Graves grew more agitated with each word.

"What about them, Mr. Graves?" asked the guide. He did not look at Graves. His eyes unnecessarily examined his perfectly manicured fingernails.

"The god-figure you praise, Kyson Jaxon Bauer, was a horrible kid. School records show that he was suspended multiple times for instigating fights, harassing female teachers and students, and using racial slurs to taunt and insult classmates. He—"

"We were talking about the animals, about the cows, Mr. Graves." He spoke to Graves like a child in time out, "What does—"

"Well, I was getting there but—"

"Of course. Now, the last time you were with us, Mr. Graves, security compelled you to leave before we entered the slaughterhouse proper. I will give them specific instructions not to for now, but you must limit your comments to those you are called on to give. I want you to be here for the whole tour. There is a special job for you at the end."

Graves said nothing. The guide smiled and recommenced his mechanical yet theatrical presentation. "Bauer killed that first sheep as a sort of prank. His thought was that whoever owned the sheep would come along and ask what he was doing and that he, Kyson Jaxon Bauer, would say that his English teacher told him to do it, or rather her poem did. While Kyson Jaxon Bauer slaughtered that first sheep, the owner of the sheep indeed happened upon the boy mid-bludgeoning. But the owner did not intervene. Rather he permitted Bauer to finish his sanguine carnage. Then, as the story goes, the owner of the sheep, a Mr. Gerald Klupke, said to Bauer, 'You shouldn't kill my sheep. I use them for wool. But I got cows, a lot of them, that I use for meat. You can kill those.'"

"The next day, Bauer and four of his teammates came to Mr. Klupke's slaughterhouse and what ensued is represented here on oil canvas. BoopBoop, a demonic deity believed to be a creation of Bauer, is said to have been witnessed by each boy present at the slaughterhouse that day. It was BoopBoop, Bauer told boys, who would sap the life essence of the cow and then impart it to the boys. The result would be heightened strength, fortitude, and senses. Please direct your attention to this painting here titled *The First Descension of BoopBoop*."

The painting was a massive oil piece, impressionist in its style, yet something about it was reminiscent of George Bellows's *Stag at Sharkey's*. Captured on this canvas were five young men, all bare head to toe, their muscles and sinews bursting in brushstrokes as they labored. Four of the boys struggled to secure each of a cow's legs. While the cow appeared to be in a fight to break loose, its face wore a look of indifference to the situation. In front of the cow stood Kyson Jaxon Bauer, a Louisville Slugger raised high in his hands. Resting in a wispy cloud above Kyson Jaxon Bauer was BoopBoop. BoopBoop, a surrealist irregularity, clashed completely with the rest of the painting. BoobBoop's skin was candy apple crimson. BoobBoop's hair was a college of cardinals. BoopBoop's ears were little speakers painted after the style of an 8-bit computer icon. BoopBoop's eyes were ping-pong balls, each with a big black X. BoopBoop's nose was silver Brazilian *bomba.* BoobBoop's open-mouth smile displayed its scattered teeth, each a pristinely sharpened pencil tip. BoobBoop's body was a single burly arm bulging with tightly sculpted flesh. BoopBoop's single hand grasped the seat of a unicycle. The unicycle was the standard type used by eccentric students on university campuses in North America.

Everyone except Graves looked at the painted BoopBoop. Many of the guests laughed and pointed. Graves heard one nearby man say to another guest, "Hell, I'd worship that little red freak if it would win me the Powerball." Both men laughed. Graves continued to stare at the floor.

The guide cleared his throat. "Now, Mr. Graves, would you please expound to the audience what happened as a result of the events captured in this piece?"

Graves raised his head and grinned, exposing his yellowed teeth and irritated gums. "Gladly. Those five kids in the painting started outperforming their teammates at practice and so the coach asks them 'hey, whaddaya guys doin' to get so strong' and Bauer says, 'we'd be happy to show you and the rest of the team.' And so, the next day, Klupke brings a few of his cows to the practice field and Bauer smacks the hell out of one's head while his buddies hold the thing down. Then one of the other players gets a turn. Next thing you know the whole team is doing it. Then after they win the state title, the town wants in on all the benefits that come from cult membership. And Klupke, he's the biggest beef producer in Missouri so he's got cows on cows on cows for these blood-thirsty little monsters."

The other guests gasped and fired dirty looks at the Graves.

One guest, a woman in her early forties, all trim and fit (everyone present except for Graves was immensely fit) and dressed in fluorescent gym apparel opened her mouth. "Bloodthirsty monsters? How dare you. Everyone here, myself included, violences animals at slaughter gyms. We are not the monsters. The monsters are the people before. The people who killed other humans. Now I don't know exactly how bad it was back then, but I read that last year there were only seven homicides in the entire country. Just seven. They don't even put violences against people in movies anymore because audiences find it too repulsive and unrealistic."

The rest of the audience rallied behind the fluorescent woman, a few people patting her on the shoulder and others letting out a *that's right* or an *uh huh.*

Graves wore a defensive expression as his posture deflated. "Well, yeah," said Graves, "but doesn't it bother you that all this so-called *progress* came from this clearly unstable and disturbed kid? I mean, the cult of BoopBoop? Really?"

"Does anyone here," asked the guide, "believe in BoopBoop?"

The audience shook their heads.

"You see, Mr. Graves, we all know the demonic god BoopBoop is fiction. We know that surrealist creature with its pencil teeth and ping-pong eyes does not hover over us as we violence animals. The movement which started with Bauer and his BoopBoop has outgrown its occult origin and blossomed into something spectacular. Something that, as this enchanting woman pointed out, has virtually erased human-on-human violence from our nation. Something that has Americans eating far less meat than before. Something that has the country in better physical condition and with a higher life expectancy than at any other point in our history. Something that has ended the abhorrent practice of factory farming and subsequently decreased our carbon emissions by astounding amounts. But why, Mr. Graves, bring up BoopBoop and the cult in your critiques? You implied earlier that what bothered *you* was the merciless and prolonged bludgeoning of animals. Do you love animals, Mr. Graves? Are you a vegetarian?"

Graves hung his head and began to slouch even more than was usual. "I'm not. But I don't eat gym-slaughtered meat. I couldn't even violence animals if I wanted to. Doctor says it's not a good idea with my heart condition. That's why I moved here. I only eat meat that comes from animals killed humanely here in the slaughterhouse."

"Indeed. The slaughterhouse," said the guide with forced joviality. "Which is why everyone is here today. To see this, the last automated animal killing facility in the country." The guide pulled a lever on the wall behind him, and two mechanical doors swung open. A small warehouse no larger than a convenience store appeared. The room was scant. A few large metal cages held seven or so cows. A sort of vise attached to a five-foot steel column rested at the center of the room. Chains hung from the ceiling directly behind the vise. Residual blood still pooled on the ground and escaped through the steel grating beneath.

The guide made his way to the steel column. He took a red handkerchief from his coat pocket and polished a corner of the vise on which he then rested his right elbow. "While the aim of this museum is to provide visitors an immersive understanding of the now outlawed factory farms of the past, we do not engage in the abuses that characterized those establishments. You'll see that all our cows have their tails. This would not be the case at a real factory farm. Their tails would be docked, or removed, to avoid tail biting, disease, and general misbehavior. Animals would also live the entirety of their life within the confines of the factory farm, never once feeling the warm solar embrace of mother nature. Not at all like our slaughter gyms where animals roam freely until the day they die."

The guide unbuttoned his suit coat to reveal a brown leather shoulder holster. From the holster he produced a slender nickel-plated pipe. "This," the guide raised the device up high, "is a captive bolt gun."

The audience inched in closer, eyeing the instrument with furrowed brows. Franklin Graves stood attentively at the front of the group, a few short feet from the guide.

"This," the guide pointed to a long trigger mechanism on the device, "will discharge the weapon and actuate the inner rod at 195 PSI. This will not kill the cow but render it unconscious and unable to feel any of the pain during slaughtering." The guide took a few steps backwards. The guests followed intently, their feet shuffling almost uniformly. The guide gestured toward the hanging chains. "The cow will then be hanged here by its hind legs, have its throat slit, and then be chopped up for Mr. Graves here to gormandize guilt-free."

Graves shuddered. He glanced at one of the caged cows. The beast chewed lazily on some hay. A churning that felt like teeth grinding on a chain link fence rattled his stomach. When Graves returned his gaze to the presentation, the guide stood inches from him.

"Here. Take it." The guide held out the captive bolt gun. "Quick and painless. I promise you the cow will feel nothing."

Graves froze. His hands remained at his side.

"Go on. Take it." The guide lifted Graves's right hand and placed the weapon in his palm. "You speak often about how this is the humane way to kill an animal. Go ahead and do it. It won't look good for your *burgeoning* career as a muckraker if you can't do the one thing you argue for."

Graves looked down at the thing. The rod was perfectly clean, reflecting the warehouse lights from its textured nickel handle. The instrument felt as though it had just been retrieved from a freezer, its cold clinging to Graves's hand, injecting ice into his veins. Graves heard cow hooves clacking on the concrete floor. He looked up from the gun. The guide positioned the cow's head in the vise and tightened the grip.

"Since Mr. Graves so favors the old ways of animal slaughtering, he will be the one to kill the bovine before you. You'll see there is a red dot on the cow's head. Place the muzzle there at a 45-degree angle and then pull the trigger. Show us all how to waste the life force of a cow." The guide raised his voice and he trembled slightly. "Show us how to make death swift, painless, meaningless, and convenient."

"So, you would rather slam the hell out of it with a baseball bat?" Graves yelled, shaking the captive bolt gun at the guide.

"*It* is a female. Clara. And yes, I would rather spend a good thirty minutes beating the life from Clara." The guide yelled now. "Because when I, when *we*," he acknowledged the other visitors, "painstakingly violence animals, we build muscle. We add something to ourselves that the cow gives us. Something more than protein. Strength. The cow gives us strength. And the cow lives on in that strength. In every lunge. In every lift. In every squat. In every step. The essence of the cow lives on as long as we do, and the image of its suffering seals their essence within us—it binds our souls. I love Clara, and I respect her enough to kill her courageously and not as a coward hiding behind the facade of convenience!" The guide breathed heavily. He produced his red handkerchief once more and wiped the sweat from his brow.

Graves said nothing. He eyed the captive bolt gun. His eyes moved from the gun to the cow. Graves stepped forward. He was next to it, to Clara. He raised the instrument up and placed the muzzle on the red dot. He closed his eyes. His trembling hand squeezed the trigger.

A scream or a wail, almost human, echoed through the warehouse. Graves opened his eyes. He had misfired the weapon. Clara flailed and twitched wildly as her crying grew louder. A chunk of her skull was removed near her eye and Graves thought he could see the pink of her brain.

"I'm sorry! I'm sorry!" was all Graves managed to say.

Four of the other guests secured each of Clara's legs and the guide released her head from the vise. "Violence her, you idiot," yelled the guide. "You did this to her. Kill her now."

"I can't—I can't."

The guide gently rested his hand on Graves's shoulder and put his lips right against Graves' ear. "You must." The guide spoke now like a priest advising through a latticed confessional wall. "She suffers. She will continue to suffer."

Graves wept. Clara's screeches rattled his eardrums. "I can't do it."

"Yes, you can." The guide put his on Graves'.

The other visitors who had secured Clara struggled now to keep her still. Several of them swore at Graves, including the florescent woman who had her arms wrapped around Clara's neck.

"You did this to her," said the guide. "Only you can set it right."

***

For eight minutes Graves bludgeoned Clara with the bolt gun. *Thump. Thump. Thump.* The first blows were coy and uncommitted—a flirtation with the force required to end life.

"You've got to want her to die!" yelled the fluorescent woman, her voice barely audible against Clara's haunting shrieks and gasps. The animal was like an endless strand of firecrackers, a whipping, writhing orchestra punctuated by staccato screeches of bludgeon percussion. Graves beat harder now. He began to hate Clara. He began to hate all the noise she made, all the suffering she manifestly emanated. It made him sick to hear her. *Thrack. Thrack. Thrack.*

"That's it!" cried the guide, tears streaking down, their salt mingling with his mustache and sincere smile.

Clara's skull collapsed. Graves saw the brain, a pinkish labyrinth of pulsing tissue. Graves tightened his grip. He beat even harder on the animal. *Sprack. Sprack. Sprack.* Only whimpers now, disoriented and without beginning or end like the sporadic hum of a failing air conditioner. *SPRACK.* No whimpers. No more breath. Clara's body teetered briefly and then fell to the ground. The sound it made was impossible to hear. Before she even reached the floor, the slaughterhouse guests erupted in claps, whistles, and cheers. Graves clutched his chest. He teetered briefly. The warehouse around him faded to blackness, the noises of the room swallowed up into a reverberating chamber of echoes and unbearably loud silence.

When his body hit the floor, it did so in two definite instances of contact. The first instance was his torso and buttocks. The second was his head. The two hit the floor at perceptibly distinct moments. Graves knew this because the sounds he heard the two sections of his body produce were separate but identical: *Boop—Boop*.

SOMETIMES YOU KILL THEM

Part I: The Letter

My Confession Letter
By Christopher Stantan

I don't like killing people. It is important to me that you know that. I've killed a lot of people, but I did not enjoy the act of taking their life. I've started to think of each murder as a reality amputation. There are some people who are finished on Earth. People who are kept here selfishly. People whose shells are a means to a profit. People who need to die but can't. So, I kill them. And everyone is happy about it—everyone except the health care companies and maybe the government. They are on their way here right now. Who knows what sort of FBI convoy is flying down 44 as I pen this?

I'm writing a confession because I know I'll be flustered when they take me in. It's probably cliche to title it "My

Confession Letter," but I did not want there to be any mistaking what it was. This is my confession. I am Murder Man.

***

In movies, when the killer comes in the darkness, they always bludgeon, or stab, or shoot the victim. That's not what I do. My work is a service to the community, so making a loud racket or leaving a bloody mess would counter my purpose. I usually just smother them. Sometimes it's as easy as turning off whatever device is keeping them alive. One flick and I'm the hero. All glory. No guts.

The first person I killed was actually a client. I'd been their insurance agent for over a decade. The wife came to me saying that some new law had been passed and that it was now illegal to discontinue care for the severely ill, including the terminally ill. I guess some daughter had sued her father for taking her mother off of life-support. The case went to the Supreme Court and was ruled in the daughter's favor. So the dad went to prison and it became criminal not to extend life.

So this client came and told me that the cost of keeping her husband, a victim of seven strokes, alive was draining all of her sanity and all of her money. The husband, a 59-year-old Social Studies teacher, was non-verbal, non-responsive, and really non-existent beyond his pulse. But there was nothing poor Maria could do. She asked if there was any way her insurance plan could be changed to decrease the cost of keeping her husband alive. I told her there was not. Poor Maria could only sit back and watch as faceless forces sucked, sucked, sucked everything up like an over-plump Dracula.

"Do you know any good real estate agents?" she asked.

"I do, but are things really that bad?"

"It's the only way I'll be able to pay for him to live. At least for a few more years. Then I don't know what we'll do." And then the soft desperation in her voice flooded over into a snotty and thick weep. "Is it evil to wish he were dead? I mean, he's not himself. He's already dead. This—this prolonging—this feels wrong."

I said nothing. I just held her hand as she sobbed.

***

Two days later I sat in Sunday school. The lesson was on the Book of Nephi, Chapter 4.

"Nephi went 'beforehand' without knowing what he was supposed to do," said the teacher. "He did not plan on killing Laban. He didn't even want to do it. But the Lord asked him to do it. So, after some resistance, Nephi took up Laban's own sword and slew him." Here, Lyle Madeira, probably my favorite Sunday school teacher, had a scriptural insight that I'd never considered. He said, "I find it significant that Nephi himself did not have a sword. He used the wicked man's own weapon to end him. And then that sword is passed down generation after generation throughout the story of *The Book of Mormon*. It's like the sword is a witness and reminder that violence should be rare and employed only when absolutely necessary, when the *Lord* deems it necessary."

The class chewed on that for a time.

An unfamiliar voice from behind me broke the silence. It was a raspy and twangy voice, the kind that sounds like it knows all the parts of a transmission and the quickest way to get anywhere. "Nephi killed that drunken Laban because they needed the brass plates, the scriptural record that they'd use to teach their children the gospel. It was an act of love for the sake of children. Killing *can* be an act of love. That's why we ought to have the death penalty for any rapist or child abuser. Plain and simple."

Lyle was thrown by the man's final statement. "Well, that's an interesting thought. But I don't think we can compare the criminal justice system to God's perfect discernment. I think He is the only one who should decide when someone is ready to leave this mortal life."

"Yessir." The unfamiliar visitor yodeled. "That's why suicide is the biggest sin of all, and all of the suicides go to outer darkness."

An audible weep escaped a voice I recognized instantly as Jennifer Saunders. It had only been a few months since her son, Eric, had taken his own life.

Lyle was visibly flustered now. "Once more, I think it is important to consider that the Savior will be the judge of all people. And he is merciful and full of love." Lyle looked at Jennifer as he said the last bit.

"Tell that to Laban," said the visitor. Then he folded his arms and was silent for the remainder of the class.

***

A week later, Maria's house sold. The two of them moved into a rental mobile home across the street from the metal recycling plant. I went to visit them. As we sat, I had to lean in to hear her over the crunch of bending and compressing copper, steel, and aluminum.

"I'm going to do it," she said. "I don't care if they lock me up. I can't do this to him. He needs to rest. Tomorrow, I'm going to have the family come over. We'll all say goodbye and then I'm pulling the plug."

The phrase hung there for a moment until it was gobbled up by a particularly nasty crunch from across the street.

"I mean isn't that murder? You could go to jail. This could ruin your life, Maria."

"What life? This is not my life. My life was growing old with my husband in my home. This is a stranger's life, and I don't care what happens to it as long as Hector is finally able to rest."

I tried to think of something to say, but the recycling plant's cacophony would not let me.

***

Maria's face shrink-wrapped to my brain. She was on every crevasse and in every little proton and neutron. Sleep eluded me. Every tick and every tock and every night sound tolled like an immense unseen bell in some dark tower that was forever away and yet right before me. But the ringing was less like a church bell. It was some other metal sound. Like a metallic crunch. So

I stared at the ceiling and waited for the tower to burst through and crunch, crunch, crunch up my soul and bones.

When I can't sleep, my wife Audrey can't sleep. She rolled over to my side of the bed.

"What are you thinking about?" she said through the darkness. Her voice banished the crunches.

I told her about Maria, about her plan.

"Is there anything you can do?" Audrey asked.

"Only one thing. Do we still have that Dread Demon costume?"

"The one Toby bought for that comic con he never went to? Yeah. It's in the unfinished basement."

"Good. I'll be back in an hour or so."

Audrey sat up in bed and embraced me. "You are a good man, Christopher. But you don't need to do this. You will still be a good man if you don't."

"I know," I said. "But I wouldn't be a good insurance agent."

***

As I drove to Maria's trailer on the other side of town, I thought about Nephi. I thought about how God guided him to kill Laban even though Nephi himself had no intention and no desire to kill the man. And now here I was, on my way to do something I'd never done and something I never wanted to do. But something within me, maybe even God, told me that this was right. And so, I drove on.

When I got to the trailer park, I donned the superhero costume. It was blood red, and it glimmered slightly in the moonlight. Recording the act was essential so that the insurance company could not pin the death on Maria or her family. So I pulled out my phone to visually document the whole thing. I hit record.

"I am…"

I had not thought out how I would narrate this evidence.

"I am going to—"

My breath escaped me.

"Just watch."

I crept into the living room window. The husband lay on his hospital bed, a breathing corpse outlined by pale refracted moonbeams. Silently, I made my way to the bedroom where I filmed Maria sleeping briefly. I was sure to capture her face in the footage. It was all very strange, but I knew exactly what to do, as though I were guided by a greater power.

I went back to the living room. I removed the man's oxygen. I grabbed a pillow with one hand while the other hand captured the deed. It was over in less than a minute. No struggle. The body seemed to welcome death. Then something happened that I had not planned for. Alarms began to beep loudly. These alarms were screaming at Maria, telling her that something was wrong with her husband. She burst into the living room while I was still making my way out the door.

As I ran to my car, Maria's cries echoed behind me. "Thank you, God," she said. "Thank you, God."

***

I mailed a disc with the video on it to the police department the next day. The next two months were a whirlwind of helping Maria navigate the health insurance company and the life insurance company. But in the end, she was able to get another home and to have enough money set aside to enjoy the rest of her life. It felt good.

But this act had made me something of a figure. I don't know who coined the name, but news outlets started to call me Murder Man. Then the tweets started. People were begging me to kill their aunts, uncles, mothers, sisters, brothers, fathers, children. So many people. So many husks.

Audrey wanted me to stop. She refused to report me, but she could not stay with me. At least that was what she said when she told me she was moving in with her parents. She still came by occasionally to check on me or to grab odds and ends, but she did not speak to me. This gave me pause. Was I crazy? Was I wrong to be helping these people? I was only giving them what they wanted, what they needed.

I prayed. I asked God what I should do. The only answer I received was, "you know what you need to do." And I did.

I've lost track now of how many people I've killed. Nobody tries to stop me. Not even police. Occasionally there will be a family member who guards the body, who thinks that what I do is immoral, or even evil. But when I arrive, they just watch. They know their desire to prolong life is just posturing and moral theatrics. In the end, they want their loved ones to be free. Isn't that what we all want? Freedom?

***

Then the insurance companies got savvy. They made a new rule: if Murder Man kills your family member, you forfeit all insurance coverage. As an insurance agent myself, I knew the companies would be sued over this and that it would be overturned eventually. Nevertheless, it scared people, and they stopped calling for me.

Then came the copycats. People dressed up as Dread Demon taking knives, guns, ropes and killing the terminally ill. They were not careful. They even killed a few innocent healthy people by accident. A new challenge faced me. I'd made this mess. I'd started this whole thing. And I did not want healthy people to die or even to get hurt. So, I decided to turn myself in.

I called the FBI this morning. I imagine they'll be here any minute. And—that's them now, I think.

Part II: The Weird Part

There's a knock. No burst through the door. No helicopters. No booming megaphones imploring me to "come out with my hands up." Just a knock.

I put the letter down and go to the door.

There's a man there. One man. He is smiling.

"Hiya! You must be Christopher Stantan."

I nod. No other communication feels possible.

"Do you mind if I come in and talk to you?"

I open the door all the way and gesture him into the living room. He sits down but then quickly gets up.

"Do you by chance have any Diet Coke? I get fidgety and just, well I'm just not myself without a little morning caffeine." He seems nervous. Not afraid nervous. But like an awkward nervous that seems to be his baseline.

"Yeah, I always have Diet Coke on hand. We don't drink coffee, so that's where we get our caffeine fix."

The man perks up at this. "Me neither. I'm a Mor—well actually we are supposed to say 'member of the Church of Jesus Christ of Latter-day Saints.'"

"No kidding? Me too. What stake are you in?" I say, and I hand him a Diet Coke.

He cracks it open, and the sound splits all the tension, breaks it into infinitesimally small bits. We are now just two Mormons shooting the breeze.

"I'm in the Saint Louis West Stake. We're in the Ellisville Ward."

"Yeah," I say. "Your Bishop, Fred Parkston and I were in Scouts together. Man, he was a little hellraiser. He made this dry ice bomb at Scout Camp one time and the thing was so loud the park ranger came down to investigate." I laugh. So does the man. The man who I only now remember remains nameless to me. "I don't think I caught your name."

He takes a long swig of Diet Coke and brings the can down to the coffee table but stops just before it touches the surface. "Do you use coasters?"

"Oh, yeah." I grab one from the end table drawer. "Here ya go."

"Thanks, Brother Stantan er—"

"Christopher is fine."

"Right, Christopher. My name is Hank Daily. We spoke on the phone this morning when you called the FBI's Saint Louis field office." Hank looks nervous again.

"Right." I let it hang there.

"Well, I just—I want to lead by saying I think very highly of what you've done. You are a good man. You are a hero. It's actually kind of like Nephi and Laban, ya know." He's fiddling with his soda can, flicking the tab up and down with his thumb. He pushes too hard and there is a little crack as the tab separates from the can. The sound startles him and he squeezes the can.

Crunch.

"Yeah. So are you going to arrest me? I kinda thought there'd be more of you."

"Um, well. No. Uh, you see—I didn't actually tell anyone you called." Hank puts the can on the coaster. "I, um—I need you to do something for me." The air shifts and we are complete strangers once more.

"What's that?"

"My wife. She, um—"

"Is she sick?"

"No. Well yes…in a *way* she is very sick." Hank is stroking his cheeks with both hands. Sweat has accumulated on his palms and forehead. He closes his eyes tightly like he just heard thunder crack right upon his own roof. Hank screams, "She has broken her covenants. She is cheating on me. She is cheating on me with a member of my ward. I saw them in our house. I saw them fornicating, Christopher. And the things? The things they were doing together? They were things I'd asked her to do for me, but she never did. She never did. She is evil, and she is destroying my life and family. She betrayed me. She betrayed her children. And she betrayed her God. And I want her to pay."

"I'm so sorry, Hank. But I—"

"You kill people. I know you do. You told me that you do. Kill her. Please, kill her."

"No. I don't kill innocent people."

"Yes, you do. They're all innocent."

"I mean, I don't kill healthy people. The people that I kill, they're already dead."

"My wife is dead. She died spiritually when she screwed Bill Weber."

"No. She can repent. She can atone."

"You are siding with that bitch? I thought you were a hero. I thought you'd understand. But you think you're better than me. I've never killed anyone. And you? You are covered in blood. Murder is murder, my friend. Nephi should have wandered without the plates, and you should have let those people suffer. But you had to do something. Your hands can't get any redder, so please just kill her and then you can be done. You're going to jail anyway." Hank pulls a pistol from inside his coat. "I can arrest you right now." Hank flicks the safety off. "Or I can say you attacked me."

"I'm sorry that your wife hurt you. But I'm not going to kill her. Why don't you just kill her?"

"I love her." Hanks gives a pitiable weep. "I can't kill her. I just want her to die." The pistol is raised, and I'm staring into the black circle at the barrel's end.

Then my eye perceives something moving behind Hank. It's Audrey. She is sneaking up behind him, and she is wielding Toby's old Louisville Slugger.

"I love her so much," Hank says again. "Please."

Like a living guillotine, Audrey swings the bat down on Hank's hand. A pistol report rattles my brain, but I feel nothing hit me. I look to the floor and see the pistol. Both Hank and I lunge for it. His lunge is interrupted by a second whack from Audrey, who nicks his head this time.

In my hands, the weapon feels like it is from another planet. I point the alien barrel at Hank. He is kneeling on the ground, blood trickling down his face like crimson tree roots. "Please, kill me. Kill me. I'm sick. I'm so sick. Kill me. I don't want to live."

The pistol feels wet and cold. My hand hates all the ridges on the handle. My hand is begging me to drop the thing to the floor. "It's not about what you want. It's about what's right." I put the gun down on the ground. "If you don't want to live, that's your choice."

Hank looks at the pistol as though it is abstract art. He picks it up, and he walks out the door, the firearm dangling loosely at his side.

"Goodbye, Hank," I say in a tired half-whisper.

Hank closes the door gently without looking back.

"He's going to be okay," I say. "Everything is going to be okay."

"We should call the police," Audrey says as she imposes her grip once more on the bat. "This all needs to end, Chris."

"Trust me, Audrey. Everything is going to be—"

A deafening pistol report comes from the front porch.

We run to the door.

On the ground lies Hank, blood gushing wildly from his gut. He's coughing, and he's writing something on the floor panels with his bloody fingers.

I AM MURDER MAN

FIXING A HOLE

Lyle Madeira did his best to ignore the buzzing of the phone in his pocket. The device seemed to be alive, rattling like a chained prisoner every minute or so. This sort of thing happened from time to time: a wild group text of his friends back in Houston talking about a trade to or from the Astros or Rockets usually being the culprit. Lyle shook his head slightly and refocused on his aloud reading of Bradbury's "Marionettes, Inc" to his students. The story chronicled the story of two men in a world where you can make mechanical replicas of yourself to do the things that you don't feel like doing. The beauty of reading this one with students was the post-reading discussion of the ambiguous ending. Lyle loved ambiguous endings, or at least he loved discussing them.

When Lyle reached the final sentences of the story, he was so entrenched in the suspense that he had not noticed that both Connors, as well as Sadie Hallstrop, were out cold while several other students were swiping through posts and messages under their desks. Lyle's voice was soft but penetrating, raspy but clear as he read those final words: "someone said."

One student, a freckle-faced girl in baggy jeans and a sweater vest, let out an audible gasp and several other students who had not been listening followed suit and produced mock surprise.

"So, the marionette version of Braling replaced the actual Braling? That's what happened, right?" asked the girl in the sweater vest, overselling her surprise with raised eyebrows and raised shoulders.

"Well, the ending is somewhat amb–"

A burst of fresh buzzes erupted from his pocket. Lyle reached in and killed the buzzing with a click.

"Ambiguous. It does seem that the marionette Braling replaced the other Braling. But what makes him the *actual* Braling?" Lyle Madeira believed the non-marionette Braling to be the true Braling, but he loved stirring the pot for the sake of discussion.

The bell rang and students rushed to the cafeteria or to a car if they were fortunate enough to have transportation for an off-campus lunch. Lyle Madeira walked back to his desk and pulled his lunch from the mini fridge. He leaned back in his office chair, sandwich in one hand and phone in the other.

"Now let's see what all the fuss was about," he said to himself, as he unlocked his phone screen.

He had received 13 texts from Nora and below that was a breaking news alert from The Associated Press. It read:

BREAKING NEWS

Global conglomerate Nile Corporation (NASDAQ:NILE) files for chapter 7 bankruptcy as several high-ranking employees confess to fraud, laundering, and insider trading. Shares plummet 99.9% as the fate of all assets and entities appears grave.

Lyle Madeira's breathing stopped. He tasted acidic vomit swelling up to his throat. He leaned over his wastebasket and retched up his breakfast along with the one ingested bite of his lunch. Lyle wiped his mouth and quickly swiped through article after article, attempting to find something hopeful, something that said Nile could lift itself up. That article did not exist. All pundits agreed that this was the end of Nile, the end of the miracle stock that had doubled in value yearly like clockwork for the last four years.

Sweat now staining the back of his shirt, hands and fingers clammy and weak, Lyle looked at the texts from Nora.

10:15 ***Did you see the news?***
10:16 ***Do we own Nile?***
10:17 ***I remember you talking to me about buying some and me saying that I was fine with it, but I don't remember if you ended up buying it or how much we bought.***

The texts went on, her anxiety building with each message. Nora had remembered that the finance app they both used was synced with their investment account. She had checked it. She had seen that the money was nearly all gone.

10:25 ***What did you do Lyle? Please tell me that money is somewhere else and that it wasn't all in Nile...***

The Madeiras had been saving for a down payment on a house for the last few years, a place with more space and a backyard for Alice and Tommy to play in. Lyle was having a surprising amount of success investing some of the down payment savings in various stocks. He had made an extra 4,000 dollars in the last nine months alone.

After reading about the annual 100% stock value increase Nile had been posting, he decided that using almost all the cash to buy up Nile could get them into a house a year earlier than they had planned. It was a high-risk move, but Nile was such a massive conglomerate, owning the largest national movie theater chain, several popular chain restaurants, a grocery store chain, a streaming service, and (most importantly) their immensely popular online retail business that sold everything from breast pumps to buck knives.

Lurching forward, Lyle Madeira vomited once more into the trash can, his body's last liquids splashing onto the sick from earlier. In a single moment, homeownership went from being two or so years away to seeming impossible.

Lyle typed out and deleted several responses before he decided that he would take the rest of the day off and talk to Nora in person. He phoned the front office and told Beth that there was a family emergency, that he would need a sub for the rest of the day. He grabbed his emergency sub plan from his desk drawer, placed it on his keyboard, and then walked briskly to his car.

No sooner than the door of his car closed did his phone begin to buzz. It was Nora, calling this time. He thought about answering for a moment but tossed the phone onto the passenger seat instead. The phone continued to buzz as he pulled out of the school's parking lot, but Lyle did not hear it.

***

Twenty-one minutes later, a black 93 Toyota Camry pulled into the parking lot of Fox Grove Apartments. In the driver's seat sat Lyle Madeira. After passing the first speed bump, he realized that he was hungry. He had tossed his breakfast, after all, and not even eaten his lunch. *Speaking with Nora on an empty stomach would only make things worse*, Lyle thought. *I'll be more agitated.* He looped around the parking lot and made his way down the road to Yumm Burger.

He ate the food in a parking spot near the end of the drive-thru, taking small bites from the paper-wrapped burger so as to prolong the meal, rehearsing in his mind the impending discussion with Nora. Some drafts of the conversation were meek and apologetic while others took a more confident approach, emphasizing that they would bounce back from all this. Each one seemed insufficient. What he truly felt like doing was weeping in her arms and saying sorry over and over again. Not even that. What Lyle actually wanted to do was crawl into a hole and stay there until he could emerge with everything fixed, everything as it was this morning before school.

Meal complete, Lyle began the drive home once more. When Keller Avenue reached their complex, he drove past. *Nora doesn't know that I took the day off*, he thought, *and I need more time to think.*

***

Ten minutes later, Lyle Madeira walked into a movie theater. He had brought the bag with his fast-food garbage from lunch, hoping to toss it in a trash can on his way in. He saw no trash can, so he shoved the paper bag into his left pocket.

The theater lobby was deserted except for a few scattered workers. Lyle bought a ticket for the 11:45 showing of the new *Ant-Man* movie. Previews had already started. Lyle made his way quickly to the podium where a theater employee waited to take admission.

The worker, an almost sickly thin middle-aged man with a wide and sincere smile, looked down at Lyle's ticket. "This one changes the whole universe. You're in for a treat," the worker told Lyle, and he tore his ticket. "Theater seven on the left."

***

Not a soul was in theater seven besides Lyle. The film had been very enjoyable so far. Great action sequences and some well-delivered humor had almost gotten his mind off of things. Just as a half-shrunken Paul Rudd shambled down the steps outside an elementary school, Lyle felt the ground below him give out slightly. There was no noise or shaking. Rather, his feet were somehow hanging now and he could not find ground with them no matter how hard he tried. Everything around him in the theater seemed normal and the movie continued to play. Lyle looked down. Past his feet, he saw a hole in the ground emitting a soft glow of light. He rubbed his eyes and looked again. The hole remained. Leaning heavily forward, Lyle attempted to get a better look into the hole. Further and further he leaned but made out nothing beyond the fact that it appeared to be a cavern of some sort. Then, leaning forward more than he realized, Lyle slipped and fell in.

To his surprise, Lyle landed on his feet. He did not dwell on the fact, and immediately he began to reach up to get back out.

"Stop! Don't move!" said a gruff and throaty voice.

Startled, Lyle stumbled forward in the direction opposite the voice.

"No! No! I told you—" the voice paused and began to pant in long raspy heaves. "I told you not to take a step and you–you took two!" the voice barked, cracking on the words *you* and *two*.

Lyle turned slowly. Though the cavern was poorly lit, Lyle made out what appeared to be the figure of a man. The figure stood against a wall that appeared to be one end of the cavern. The figure wore a paper bag on his head, concealing his face.

"Don't do anything rash," Lyle pleaded to the figure. "I'm just going to get up out of here. I won't tell anyone that you're down here. It will be like this never happened." Lyle began to lift his hands once more.

"No! No! No! You can't! No!" the figure cried, wretched and feeble, reaching out his hand.

Lyle stopped. "Please, just let me go. I don't know what any of this is and I don't care. I just—"

"Your name is Lyle Pinto Madeira." The figure began to slouch now, and his voice was soft but penetrating. Each word was as clear as it could be through the figure's wavering breaths. "You were born in Belo Horizonte, Brazil. You moved to Houston before you can remember. You are in trouble right now. Not with me. Financial trouble. You invested almost all of your down payment savings in Nile stock, and now it's gone."

"Who told you all of that? What are you going to do?"

"I don't *do* anything. I *can't*. I remain here. If you want to be with your family again, you need to listen to me right now. Do not interrupt me and do not ask me any questions. Understand?"

Lyle nodded slowly.

"This tunnel is a one-way tunnel. You can only walk in that direction." The figure pointed away from the wall of the cavern that was directly behind him. "Go ahead. Try to step toward me."

Lyle lifted his right foot, but his knee immediately bumped into something. Reaching out, he felt the rough dampness of a cave wall separating himself from the figure. But Lyle did not see the wall he felt.

"Take another two steps away from me but only two," the figure said.

Lyle did so. When he reached once more toward the figure, Lyle felt that the invisible wall had moved with him. "What is th—"

"No questions and no talking. Now, look at the walls and ceiling of the tunnel. Take your time observing them."

Lyle inspected the walls and ceiling carefully. Each revealed a slightly blurred image of what seemed to be a screen in a movie theater. Looking even closer, Lyle perceived that the film on the screen was the *Ant-Man* sequel.

"Now, be careful to not move your feet from where they are," the figure said, "but lean forward as much as you can without taking a step and look at the wall as you do so."

As Lyle leaned forward, Paul Rudd moved in reverse, taking a step backwards up the steps of the school. Lyle repeated the motion, and like a looped video, Paul Rudd would go forward and backwards slightly with each lean.

"You see, Lyle, every step that you take in this cavern is a step backwards in time. If you had enough provisions, you could travel years into the past. As you travel forward into the tunnel, you will see on the walls whatever you, Lyle Madeira, were seeing at that moment in the past. A hole to leave the tunnel will appear when you reach up to the ceiling but *don't* do that until you are absolutely certain that you want to leave. You can only open one hole. And you either leave through that hole or another you comes in through that hole."

"Another me?"

"Yes. There will be another you from the past waiting on the other side of that hole, and only one of you can travel through the hole."

The figure was speaking rapidly now, and although his speech continued in a whisper, his frustration mounted. "I told you not to take a step when you entered because had you remained where you were when you landed down here, you could have gotten up and left like nothing happened. But you ruined that. If you were to reach up now, you would encounter yourself watching a movie in the theater and would thus be in a very difficult situation."

Lyle's mouth gaped, his expression somewhere between disbelief and fear. *How could there be another Lyle? Lyle is me. I am me.*

"Now," the figure continued, "you can go as far back in time as you would like, but I recommend leaving the tunnel while the Lyle Madeira on the other side is sleeping. You will be able to tell he is sleeping because his dreams will show on the walls of the tunnel." The figure gestured to the walls with all the rehearsed banality of a flight attendant delivering preflight instructions.

"Once you are ready to leave the tunnel, you are faced with a choice: you can assume an alias and start a new life in the past or you can kill the iteration of yourself that is living in the past into which you enter. If you do not kill him then you will not be able to have the life you knew. You will not be a teacher at Hillcrest High School. You will not be married to Nora. You will not be the father of Alice and Tommy. The *other* Lyle Madeira will be those things." Everything was explained so matter-of-factly as though the figure was reviewing aloud a syllabus on the first day of class.

"But won't—"

The figure raised his hand and his voice. "For the last time, no talking and no questions!"

After several labored breaths, the figure began to speak again.

"The choice is yours. Once you exit the tunnel, the hole will close, and you will not be able to reopen it. At this moment, I would turn around and start walking if I were you."

Finished with his lecture, the figure took over a minute to sit down, making sure not to move forward in the tunnel at all. He groaned and winced with each adjustment of his arms and legs, but eventually sat down, legs crossed on the tunnel floor.

"Who are you and why are you helping me?" Lyle asked.

The figure let out a howl like the tearing of the sky and pounded his chest with immense force. It reverberated in deafening waves off the walls of the cavern. In the same instant that the figure hit his own bosom, a painful blow to his own chest sent Lyle stumbling backwards and away from the figure.

"Go now!" yelled the figure, his command echoing down the tunnel.

Lyle began to sprint, images on the walls and ceiling moving rapidly in reverse all around him as he ran. At first, Lyle could hear the figure's sobs as he ran, but after a minute only the pitter-patter of his own footfalls filled the cave. He did not stop sprinting until he reached the point in the tunnel where the wall bore an image of himself reading the Associated Press alert on his phone.

***

Lyle Madeira sat himself down against the wall of the tunnel. Panting heavily, he attempted to make sense of the impossible everything that had been the last 30 minutes. Or had it been 30 days? He could not tell. It was all ridiculous. Yet, everything that the figure told him had been true so far. The tunnel functioned just as he explained it would. As Lyle stared at the news alert on the wall, he thought of how inconsequential the lost money now seemed. The warning that the figure gave him stained his thoughts: *If you do not kill him then you will not be able to have the life you have known.*

The thought of not being able to hold Nora, Alice, and Tommy made Lyle feel hollow and frail like a discarded snakeskin husk. Worse still was the fact that there would be another Lyle Madeira who would get to live out his days with Nora and the kids.

The other Lyle would watch Alice's soccer games, build Lego empires with Tommy, and watch reruns of *The Office* with Nora after the kids were asleep. The other Lyle would walk Alice down the aisle, retire with Nora and spend the last years of their lives seeing the world together and spoiling their grandchildren. All the familiar episodes of a well-lived American life. Each thought was more sickening than the last.

Lyle willed himself to dwell on those possibilities no longer. He himself was Lyle Madeira. If he killed the other Lyle, the death would be sudden. Over and done. But if he let the other Lyle live then he himself would be eternally burdened with the knowledge of the life he lost. A life without his family was no life at all.

Yet there was a chance that after a conversation the other Lyle could be persuaded to share Nora, Tommy, Alice, and the rest of his life. They could take turns. One day on and one day off. He remembered the twins played by Christian Bale in *The Prestige*. They shared the life of a single man. *It worked for them, didn't it?* he thought. He had not seen the film for some time and could not remember if it did.

Lyle imagined himself approaching the other Lyle, explaining the whole mess, and making the proposition. He imagined being the other Lyle. Would he accept? No. He would not believe any of it, and he would probably call the police—or worse.

If he did kill the other Lyle, nobody in his family would ever know. To them, everything would be just as it had always been. Like nothing happened. Yes, he was not about to lose his family because fortune had thrown him into some absurd hole. He would kill the other Lyle. That he accepted it so quickly sent a pillar of ice through Lyle's core, the guilt of the act already plaguing his conscience.

Lyle looked to the ceiling of the cavern and began to sob. The light from the Associated Press alert reflected a faint red in his tears as they ran down his cheeks and onto his quivering lips. The salty taste of the warm tears comforted him. He cried more and licked up all the tears.

***

It was time to move. Lyle had only traveled about two hours into the past so far and he intended to travel three days total. The clock on his phone seemed to be working still. Lyle began to run once more, but this time he glanced continually back and forth between the clock on his phone and the clock on the wall of his classroom. After tracking the two for five minutes in tunnel time, Lyle reckoned that it took him about five minutes of running to travel 30 minutes into the past. If he kept a good pace, he could reach his desired exit point in about a day and a half tunnel time.

As he jogged, he plotted how he would kill the other Lyle. He was disgusted at how easy it was for himself to throw around countless scenarios in which he took the other Lyle's life. Maybe this was the survival instinct that had led so many of the characters in the novels he taught to commit their heinous deeds. Naturalism. *No*, he thought, *this is Surrealism.*

First, Lyle imagined shooting the other to oblivion with a shotgun so that nobody could recognize the corpse. In this scenario, he would tell everyone that it was a violent home invasion and that he acted in self-defense. He immediately discarded the idea as it had too many loose ends. What if they ran DNA tests and found out they were the same person? People would also be very suspicious of the fact that the intruder had been shot so many times. And most importantly, Lyle did not own a shotgun or any gun for that matter.

Several other possibilities were explored, but most were impossibilities requiring both Lyles to be somewhere unique like a lake or a ravine. Lyle had limited time to execute the plan and would have to work with locations where the other Lyle would naturally be alone. All at once, the perfect plan came to him. Lyle saw how he would kill his copy. Then he leaned over and retched. Nothing came out.

On the Sunday night three days past, Nora, Alice, and Tommy were at Lyle's in-laws'. Lyle had been behind on grading essays, so he stayed home to work. The plan was to sneak into the apartment and use a rope to strangle the other Lyle from behind. If he did it quickly, there would be no signs of a struggle. Quick and clean.

The plan was foolproof. He would have his family and, what's more, he would be able to sell all the shares of Nile before the collapse. Though the thought of strangling a copy of himself (or anyone for that matter) repulsed him, losing his family would be a fate worse than death. Their faces flashed across Lyle's mind. His longing to be with them quickened his pace.

***

More than a day of tunnel time had passed. Lyle was thirsty, hungry, and fatigued. Though he slowed his pace a few times, Lyle had moved continually since he left the point of the tunnel with the phone alert. He sat down to rest. *Just a short breather*, he thought. Moments later he succumbed to a deep and dreamless sleep.

When he came to, he grabbed his phone in frantic haste to check the time. Lyle had slept for 12 hours. Initially, he was worried that he had somehow lost time by sleeping so long, but the wall before him still displayed Lyle and Tommy playing with blocks on Sunday afternoon.

Lyle heaved himself up and continued his journey. Though he had slept long, he did not feel rested in the slightest. Likewise, he had no more hunger or thirst than he did before his rest. But these facts were hardly strange when placed next to the fact that he was in a cave walking backwards through time.

Five tunnel hours later, Lyle arrived at the spot where he planned to exit into the past. The walls and ceiling revealed a still of a dream Lyle had Saturday night in which he and Nora were in college again taking a pencil sharpening class. He only remembered having the dream after seeing it play out in reverse on the wall. At the current location of the tunnel, the wall wore a still shot of a monocle sporting professor with a soul patch inspecting Lyle's freshly sharpened pencil.

Lyle took a deep breath and reached for the ceiling of the cave. He looked up. The wooden slats of a bed frame could be seen through the hole. With hyper deliberateness, Lyle inched his way up in soundless micromovements until he was lying prone beneath the bed where Nora and the other Lyle slept. He thought briefly about switching to a more comfortable position but abandoned the idea for fear of making noise or bumping the bed frame.

Unaware of exactly how many hours until morning, Lyle passed the time walking through all the steps of his plan. At one point, he bumped the bed frame while stretching his neck. Someone shifted above him but remained blissfully oblivious to the guest beneath.

Gradually, the floor beyond the bedframe transitioned from black to tawny gray and then to the first golden hues of a sunny morning. Had he climbed out into a weekday or even a Saturday morning, both Nora and the other Lyle would be up already, but they liked to sleep in as much as possible on Sundays.

Eventually, the two of them rose and made their way down the hall to the kitchen. As soon as he heard the clanking of dishes, he moved quickly to make his escape. He slid his head out from under the bed, eyeing the bedroom's sliding glass door that opened to a balcony. As Lyle slid, something stopped his head. He looked up. 19-month-old Tommy stared down at him.

"Daddy!" he squealed in delight. Tommy was handsome, tall, and muscular for a toddler. People were always struck by his size and by how fast he sprinted across rooms. His eyes were a deep blue, and his nose housed a large birthmark. When Tommy was first born, Lyle would put his thumb over the birthmark sometimes to see what his son's face would look like without the large brown splotch. But after months of holding him, kissing him, tickling him, and cradling him in the late hours of whimper-filled nights, the mark seemed to disappear. It was no longer some spot on his son. It was simply a natural part of the beautiful little boy who he loved entirely.

Lyle got to his feet quickly, gave Tommy a kiss on the forehead, and made his way to the sliding door. Tommy followed.

"Daddy! Daddy!" he repeated as he trailed Lyle.

"Daddy's here in the kitchen, sweetie," Nora called. "Come here."

Lyle began to slide open the door slowly.

Tommy shambled over to the partly open door and attempted to go outside, one of his favorite activities. Lyle gently pushed Tommy away. Tears pooled in Tommy's eyes. The child made the familiar prolonged inhale that preceded a tantrum. A wail erupted from Tommy. Lyle looked into his son's crying eyes. He wanted to tell the boy he loved him, to hold him, to take him outside and watch him throw mulch chips onto the cool morning pavement. *Maybe later*, Lyle thought.

That *maybe* choked him. Cold hands emerged from somewhere deep inside him, squeezed his throat, his whole body until Lyle could hardly see little Tommy who stood only inches away. Lyle threw the door open and shut it behind himself in two swift motions, pushing Tommy back all the while. Then he hopped down to the grass and sprinted away from the building. Tommy's muffled cries of *Daddy, Daddy* faded behind him as he ran.

***

Five blocks from the apartment complex sat a bridge. The bridge crossed Oakdale Creek. Before the construction of the bridge, the area underneath the old bridge had been a preferred haunt of vagrants. Four years ago, however, the area was closed off for almost a year during the construction of the new bridge. The vagrants vanished and never returned. Under the bridge, Lyle could hear cars zoom past. Occasionally he heard the conversations of passing pedestrians, some of them familiar neighborhood voices. The brush that surrounded the bridge was so dense that no passerby could see Lyle unless they went beneath themselves.

Lyle opened the investment app on his phone to schedule a market sale of all his Nile shares. When he tried to open the app an error message appeared on his phone.

Connectivity Error:
Duplicate SIM card detected. Please contact your service provider.

With no internet access on his phone, Lyle would have to use free wifi at some public place. On the off chance that someone he knew would see him and report location inconsistencies to Nora, Lyle did his best to disguise himself. He dirtied his face and clothes with mud from the creek. The intention was that he would look like a homeless person. The result was that he looked like a person who had fallen into a puddle of mud. All the same, when Lyle looked at his reflection on the phone screen, he was not immediately recognizable.

Costume complete, Lyle Madeira made his way to the Fast Mart two blocks away. He hid behind a stack of wood pallets in the back alley of the building. The signal was faint, but Lyle was able to connect to the Wi-Fi and open the app once more. This time the app itself gave an error alert.

Error:

This device is not registered to be used with account "lyle.madeira909." Select "send" to deliver a one-time verification code to the phone number on the account.

A few months back Lyle had required all new logins to the investment app to be approved by a text sent to his phone. For some reason, this copy of the phone had been logged out of the app. There was no way the other Lyle would approve some random login attempt.

Lyle's mind raced. Then Lyle remembered that the other Lyle would be dead soon. With his doppelganger gone, Lyle would be able to use that copy of his phone to sell the shares.

Blood money. His blood. Innocent blood. Lyle tried to shake the murder thoughts and all the sickness that accompanied them. The more he thought about it, the physics and biology of it, the more unsure he was of his capacity to take human life. *How do you kill another man?* The question was not one of method but of mental fortitude. *How?*

He thought, as he often did, about the characters in the stories he taught his students. He thought about the Misfit killing the grandma in the O'Connor story. The Misfit killed the woman because he had felt threatened by something in her, something sickening but disguised as love. Something beautiful and hideous.

But the Misfit found no pleasure in the deed. What was it he had said at end about life being without pleasure? Like O'Connor's antagonist, Lyle too felt that had his life been different, he would not have to be a killer. It was the unfair falling of the chips that compelled the Misfit to be a murderer. Fate dealt likewise to Lyle, and what was he to do? Kill another Lyle? No. He could not think like that. It was not killing. It was rebalancing the cosmic scale thrown off by that damn hole in that damn theater. Lyle was the protagonist. He had to be.

***

Around 5 pm, Nora, Alice, and Tommy left the apartment to go to Lyle's in-laws. They would not return until 8 pm or so. At 6 pm, Lyle Madeira exited the cover of the bridge in the direction of Fox Grove Apartments. He had purchased a utility rope at the Fast Mart. There had been two options: a four-dollar rope and a twenty-five-dollar rope. Lyle had never killed anyone with a rope. He did not want to gamble on cheap rope. The rope, now tucked into the back of his pants, remained sealed in plastic packaging.

Almost half an hour later, Lyle was on the patio outside of his and Nora's bedroom. His hope was that it would still be unlocked from this morning. It was. He took a deep breath and slid the door open slowly. He could hear the TV and knew for a fact that the other Lyle was in front of it, grading essays. He began to creep into the hall. He reached for the rope. His fingers touched the plastic wrapping. Opening the plastic would not be a quiet affair.

Lyle returned slowly to the bedroom and went into the small master bath to open the rope. He went to put the wrapping into his left pocket, but the paper bag from Yumm Burger was still there. He shoved the wrapping into his right pocket instead. Lyle then wrapped the rope around each of his hands several times as he had seen done in movies.

Lyle left the bedroom once more. He inched his way down the hall, only thinking about the next footstep, trying not to imagine the act at the end of his path.

The other Lyle sat beneath him, absorbed in the essay glowing on his laptop screen. Viggo Mortenson glowed on the television screen, addressing an army of green ghosts. Lyle reached toward himself. His hands trembled, making the rope rattle like an injured snake. Lyle watched his hands lower the rope. Then the other Lyle's phone rang. It was a video call from Nora. Lyle ducked quickly behind the couch. How could he have forgotten about the call? Alice had lost a tooth at her grandparents' house and called Lyle to tell him.

The conversation was brief. At the end, Alice said, "I love you so so much, Daddy! And I wish you were here! You'll make sure the tooth fairy comes tonight, right? Last time the tooth fairy was a day late, and you said you'd remind her for my next tooth."

"I wish I was there too, sweetie," said the other Lyle. "I love you. And of *course* I'll make sure the tooth fairy comes. Bye-bye."

Alice said her goodbye and blew a kiss which the other Lyle returned. The call was over. Once more it was just the two of them. The other Lyle unmuted *The Return of King* and resumed his grading.

He loves her, he thought. *He loves her just as much as I do.* Lyle's grip on the rope loosened.

A thud came from the bedroom. The other Lyle got up quickly to investigate and somehow did not see a perfect copy of himself hiding behind the couch. In a breathless flash, Lyle ran to the front door and left the apartment.

***

Cars zoomed over the bridge above. Lyle Madeira wept, tears painting wet streaks into the dried mud on his cheeks. *I can't kill him*, he thought. *I don't want to kill him. I just want my family back. I just want my family back. I just want my family back.*

The rest of that night was a mixture of weeping for what was lost and plotting miracles. Miracles consisting of scenarios in which Lyle could be with his family again without committing murder. Of course, he thought about going back to the theater on Tuesday and entering the hole once more, but that would be pointless. There would still be another Lyle living with his family wherever he came back out, and Lyle knew he could not kill him. Mostly because he knew it was wrong and partly because he felt incapable of taking life.

There was one scenario, however, where Lyle would not have to kill anyone and he could be with his family again. It was possible that some years down the road, the other Lyle would get into a fatal car accident or something of the like. If Lyle spent his life following the other Lyle as closely as possible, he could switch out his body for the deceased Lyle and everything would be back to normal for him. Though he felt macabre wishing for a natural turn of events to kill the other Lyle, he felt better about wishing for that than he did about killing.

So if he was to wait for the other Lyle to die, what would he himself do in the meantime? He could not exist as himself. He could not go to his job or even use any of the IDs or credentials possessed by the other Lyle. He could not commit to a new career. He had to be ready at any point to replace the other Lyle. He would have to follow the other Lyle like a shadow. So many thoughts and all of them providing no path, no solution.

Lyle wanted a break from thinking. He swiped his phone open and went to his news app. The page had not refreshed since before falling into the tunnel. All the articles were those of two days in the future from the current time. There were scores for baseball and basketball games, stocks that rallied over the last week, and various other future events. If he could get his hands on some capital. If he placed a few bets and shorted a bunch of NILE, he could make a small fortune. He could live comfortably as he spends his days tracking the other Lyle and waiting for a catastrophe.

It was too late now to take any action. Tonight, he would rest under the bridge as Lyle. The real Lyle. Tomorrow he would become a ghost of himself, a lingering spirit waiting for the opportunity to creep back into his own life. He did not think of killing anyone for the rest of the night, and though it was cold and rocky under the bridge, Lyle could not remember a better night's sleep.

***

In the morning, the putt-putts and screeching brakes of morning's commuters woke Lyle. He stood up, rubbed the sleep from his eyes, and made his way to the Fast Mart for breakfast. He had four dollars cash remaining and would need to execute his plan quickly today if he wanted to eat tomorrow.

Lyle snatched a banana, a big fountain cup of water, and a little bag of crackers. He placed all his intended purchases on the counter and waited for the cashier to scan them. The cashier did not scan them. Instead, he stared open-mouthed at Lyle.

"Hey, you look just like that guy," the cashier said.

Lyle froze. He managed to get out the words "what guy?"

"The guy on TV," said the cashier, and he pointed up to a mounted television. "Too bad yer not him. The dude just won the Powerball. 235 million bucks!"

Lyle looked at the television. Smiling on the screen, holding both Alice and Tommy with Nora at his side, stood the other Lyle.

The cashier watched a few more moments of the news story and then turned to scan Lyle's purchases, but Lyle was gone.

***

How was this possible? Lyle asked himself over and over as he made his way back to the bridge. *I never buy lottery tickets, and I know that I didn't win the lottery today because I've already lived it.* Lyle stopped walking. He looked down at his feet. A manhole lay beneath them. Lyle observed the manhole. He imagined a hand reaching out from whatever lay beneath it. The hand looked familiar. He furrowed his brow and clenched his teeth. Rage swelled deep within him like an atomic volcano ready to wipe away all existence. Lyle took a long and deep breath. Then he began to sprint.

***

The bushes on the south side of his in-law's house provided plenty of cover for Lyle. The lotto-winning Lyle and his family would be there at some point today to celebrate. His only hope was to catch the other Lyle alone outside. After an hour of waiting, Nora and the kids pulled into the driveway. Lyle's mother-in-law sprinted to the car to greet them.

"I still can't believe it," she said, and she broke out into tears of joy as they all walked inside.

A few hours later, the other Lyle arrived. It was darker now. A purple-blue twilight framed the scene. Lyle removed himself from the bushes, the rope wrapped tightly around each hand. He crept toward the other Lyle, his face contorted with hatred. The other Lyle took slow steps. His posture sagged. His hands were dark with dirt and dried mud. Just as he was within reaching distance, Lyle stepped on a stick—the crack fissuring time and space and reality.

"I know you're there," the other Lyle said softly as he stopped. "Just do it."

"You. You killed him. The other one. Didn't you?" Lyle whispered vehemently.

"You already know the answer to that." The other Lyle paused. "I don't care anymore. I don't care as long as one of us is with them. To help them. To keep them—"

Lyle lunged and wrapped the rope tightly around the other Lyle's throat. He yanked the murderer to the ground and proceeded to throttle him. The copy made no attempt to stop Lyle. No counter-offensive. He tried only to speak.

"I—thought I was—I thought," the other Lyle rasped. "I—I thought—I was the—"

Lyle pulled even tighter. There was no more talking. Moments later, the other Lyle was dead.

Exhaling for the first time since the attack ensued, Lyle dropped the rope. The panic of being discovered by his family set in immediately. He did not even remark that he had killed a man. There was no time. Acting in manic haste, Lyle grabbed the keys from the pocket of the corpse, threw the body into the back of his car, and left the house without looking back. Lyle knew exactly where to take the body. There was a hill to the east of the city limits. He went there sometimes when he needed to be alone. In all his trips to the hill, he had never seen another soul.

Lyle pulled his car over onto a gravel road near the hill. It was darker now but still light enough to make out the shapes of tree trunks in the forest before him. He worked his way through the woods, dragging the body with two hands as he walked backwards.

Arriving at the spot where the forest met the eastern foot of the hill, Lyle dropped the body. *Damn it*, he thought. Lyle had no shovel. He kneeled and began to dig with his bare hands.

After only seconds of hand shoveling, his fingertips struck something solid but much softer than rock. Lyle began to clear the dirt away. His face contorted, and he jolted to his feet, covering his mouth.

A familiar face looked up at him from the dirt. Lyle's hand trembled as it activated the flashlight on his phone. The cool white LED confirmed what he had already known to be true. The face looking up at him from the dirt was his own. He observed the area around him. Innumerable mounds of dirt spanned the forest floor.

Lyle's gaze steadily moved from the forest floor to his left pocket. He reached in and pulled out the paper bag from Yumm Burger.

***

He had been right about the cosmic scales being off balance, but he had no idea to what extent this new reality was warped. Nora nestled against him in bed. "I've never made love to a millionaire before," she had told him earlier as she pulled off his clothes, the clothes that Lyle had taken from a dead man only hours before.

"Me neither," Lyle had responded. It was the sort of thing he knew he would usually say in that moment, but the joke came out flat.

Nora did not notice. Her unbridled effervescence overtook her and managed to eventually overtake Lyle.

She now lay sleeping inches from him. This should be the victory. This should be the end of it. But it was not. Lyle could not stand to lie in the bed. He knew what could be under there, what may be under there at that very moment.

After Nora had been asleep for about a half-hour, Lyle rolled silently from their mattress. He stood for a moment looking at the edge of the bed frame. Then in one swift motion, he got on one knee and looked under the bed. Nothing.

Relief. But it was only momentary. *I need to get somewhere with people, people who are awake.* He went quickly to his car, watching the ground below him the whole time.

Once in the car, he realized that a copy could come out from under the car at any moment of his drive. He watched the rearview mirror as he drove, looking at the road sporadically. Yet for the entire drive, no other Lyle appeared.

***

The Denny's was empty at this hour except for one table of high school kids in the far corner. The hostess began to walk Lyle to a booth on the side of the restaurant opposite the teenagers, but Lyle stopped her.

"Could I sit over there, please?" he asked, pointing over toward the kids.

She looked at Lyle and then at the chortling high schoolers. They were filling the soda in front of an empty seat with salt and sweetener. The hostess rolled her eyes and led Lyle to a booth near the group.

"Actually, could you put me at a table with chairs?" Lyle asked.

"Just sit wherever you want, okay," the hostess said, and she walked away.

Lyle sat at the table closest to the kids. He was safe now. He could plot his next move, his final move to rebalance this mess the cosmos had thrust upon him.

"Mr. Madeira?" One of the teenagers said. "Hey, it's Madeira! So, you gonna quit teaching, Mr. Millionaire?"

They were all his students. He knew it for a fact, and yet they seemed completely unrecognizable. Lyle never forgot a student's name, and here he was next to four strangers he knew very well. Lyle heard himself say something that was apparently witty because the students all cracked up, one of them saying, "So it's like that, huh?"

Then, to Lyle's relief, the students returned to their own world and left him to think. The plan was simple. It came to him all at once, clear and bright like a holy vision. All he would need was a gun.

But where do you get a gun? Guns require permits and background checks. Yet, crazy people were killing people with guns all the time. There had to be somewhere he could get one last minute. *Wait, I'm a millionaire*, he thought. *I can get whatever I want.*

The students were getting up to leave. Lyle stood up to follow them out, the pancakes he ordered still on the kitchen griddle. The students exchanged strange glances as they peeked back at Mr. Madeira, who appeared to be following them. The group, whose noise in the restaurant moments before had measured on the Richter scale, now walked in silence.

A collective sigh of relief came over all of them when Mr. Madeira went to the other side of the parking lot. The sigh was short-lived. Mr. Madeira's tires screeched like Jurassic Park raptors as the teacher peeled out, narrowly missing the students.

***

Lyle had never bribed anyone, nor had he ever committed a crime, unless killing a copy of yourself was a crime. If it was then Lyle was about to commit his second crime. He stared at the glass case of firearms in the sporting section of the Walmart.

As luck would finally have it, there was a very rough and very desperate-looking worker behind the counter. The worker's hair was a long blonde greasy mop that hung to his shoulders. Ink dragons and skulls ran the length of his forearms up to the rolled-up sleeves of his plaid shirt. The few teeth that he had were yellowing and he smelled of tobacco and pet urine. The nameplate attached to his blue vest had "Dane" scribbled in black permanent marker.

"Hi, there. I'd like that pistol right there, please," Lyle said. In front of him lay dozens of pistols in a glass counter display.

"Which pistol?" Dane asked.

Lyle pointed at one that was not too small but not too big, the Goldilocks of handguns he thought.

"That one?" the worker asked, pointing at a different gun.

"Yeah, that one." The pistol was matte dark gray and significantly larger than the one Lyle wanted. Yet, he assumed they would all do the same thing and bigger was always better, right?

The worker unlocked the case, pulled out the gun, and handed it to Lyle who looked unsure of how to hold the thing.

"Uh, there's the safety n' yeah that should be good. You needin' ammunition tonight?"

"Um, yes. A case, please."

"Jacketed or lead?"

Lyle did not know the difference. He asked for lead.

The worker bent down and disappeared. Seconds later he reemerged with a red and brown box that jingled slightly when he set it on the glass counter.

"That'll be $424.24," Dane said.

Lyle handed him the credit card. Was he not going to ask Lyle to see his permit or whatever it was? No wonder people were getting shot up at schools and malls and every other day. Lyle had to remind himself that this was a fortunate occurrence, but he could not help but feel contempt for the man. A few moments later, Dane handed Lyle his card back. After sliding the card back into his wallet, Lyle grabbed the bag.

"Sir, before you can take that, I need to see yer permit n' ID."

Lyle, half thankful that they did indeed ask for this and half furious that he could not just stroll on out with his new pistol, looked up at Dane who had now placed his hand on the shopping bag.

"Let me get that for you," Lyle said. His body temperature rose as he pretended to search for the nonexistent permit. He felt sweat accumulating on his forehead and back. The beads of perspiration were itchy and cold as they ran down his spine. "You know," Lyle began as he gave up his fictitious search, "I must have lost it somewhere in the store. I know for a fact that I had it."

He let the statement hang there, and he waited to see what the worker would do. After looking Lyle up and down for a few seconds, the look on the worker's face shifted in a single explosion of facial contortions.

"Yer that guy!" he yelled. "Yer that guy who won the lottery aren't you?"

Lyle gave a tiny nod with a tight-lipped smile. He began to look around to see if anyone else was around that had heard the worker. They seemed to be alone in this part of the store.

"Man, I wish I had yer luck. Damn. 89 million, right? Damn. Well, unfortunately, I can't let ya take the gun without a permit. But I'll keep it here for ya until ya come back." The worker was chummy now, as if Lyle had purchased many guns from him during many other night shifts before this.

"Look, we are leaving town early in the morning and I need this gun to give to my father as a gift." Lyle could not believe how easily the lie came into existence and spilled off his lips simultaneously. "Tell you what. If you do me this favor, I'll give you ten thousand dollars, and I'll bring you the permit when we get back from our trip. I mean, what's ten thousand to me now?" Lyle forced a laugh.

"Damn. You've been rich for not even a day and ya already think you can buy me? Do I look like a criminal to you?" Dane asked.

Lyle's first thought was *yes,* but he did not say this. "Fifty thousand. Give me your address, and I'll have it there as soon as I get my money."

The worker grabbed a pen, scribbled his address on the back of Lyle's receipt, and handed the receipt to Lyle. "Go now. But if they link me to whatever it is yer doin', I will rat you out. I'll blackmail you, understand?"

"You got it," Lyle said, and he stuffed the receipt in his pocket and began to walk briskly out of the store. Even at this hour, a greeter stood at the exit and gave Lyle a friendly goodbye.

As he stepped out into the solitary night, Lyle observed that he was alone walking in the parking lot. He ran to his car. Then he roared out of the parking lot, disappearing into the darkness.

***

He spent the rest of the night taking only right turns and only stopping once to fuel up. He had quickly slid the fuel pump into the tank, pulled the trigger on the pump, and then fell to his knees. *Nothing under the car.* Lyle was breathing heavily. He stood back up and spread his legs wide, looking down at the ground until the metal click told him his tank was full.

As he pulled away, Lyle saw that the ground where his car had been parked was empty. He exhaled and made the first of many more right turns.

***

The streets, empty and serene, were painted rose gold by electric light, but their tranquility and beauty offered no peace to Lyle. At any moment a copy or multiple copies for all he knew could emerge from the shadows and overtake him.

He reached for his pistol. The cold metal made him feel sick. He did not care for guns. This one in particular felt heavy, but maybe it was light. He had no frame of reference.

Lyle drove for the next few minutes with the pistol in his lap, the handle nestled in his right hand. *How do you load one of these things?* he thought.

Lyle had seen it done in movies and TV so many times but had no idea where to start with the whole process. Lyle set the gun back on the passenger seat, checked his rearview mirror for the 49th time that minute, and made a right turn. With the phone he grabbed off the other Lyle, which he now imagined had been nicked off countless other Lyles, he looked up a video of how to load a pistol.

He had right turned his way into a small neighborhood with few street lights. His heart began to race. The next three minutes were spent frantically darting his eyes from the gun, to the video, to the road, to the rearview mirror, to the left, to the right, to the gun again, to the video. He was finding it hard to see exactly what the video was showing him, so he pulled the phone closer to his face.

"At this point, you should already have your magazine loaded," the woman in the video said. "Take the magazine and—"

THUD

Lyle stopped the car. Unloaded pistol in hand, he flung himself out of the car and walked slowly around to the back of the vehicle.

A large dog, a black and brown mutt with no collar, lay on the ground motionless.

"I'm sorry," Lyle whispered, and he wept.

***

Wild and paranoid as he was for the rest of the night, nobody and nothing came to get Lyle.

He pulled into the driveway at 6:30 am.

Nora was already up cooking breakfast. She asked where he had been.

He said that he could not sleep, which was true.

She smiled and told him that she understood.

He was thankful she did not.

They shared breakfast before Alice and Tommy were up. He made up a story about having to go and sign a bunch of paperwork at the bank and told her he needed to take the day off.

She laughed. "Lyle, you can take the rest of your life off." She smiled and kissed him. As they kissed, he remembered that today was the day that Nile's stock would tumble. That money seemed pointless now next to their fortune, next to their life together.

Lyle pulled Nora closer.

***

The theater lobby was deserted except for a few scattered workers. Lyle bought a ticket for the 11:45 showing of the new *Ant-Man* movie. Previews had already started, so Lyle made his way quickly to the podium where a worker was stationed to take admission.

The same thin middle-aged employee with a wide and sincere smile looked down at Lyle's ticket just as he had before. "This one—"

"Changes the whole universe," Lyle interrupted. "You have no idea."

The admissions worker gave Lyle the torn ticket and a weird look. He opened his mouth to speak, but Lyle spoke first.

"Theater seven on the left."

***

The theater was empty. Lyle made his way to the exact seat he had been in before. Lyle pulled the pistol from the back of his pants and sat down. He switched the safety off and waited. His eyes never once left the floor to watch Paul Rudd shrink or grow, except for when the schoolhouse scene started. *This is it*, he thought, and he looked back down to the floor.

The hole appeared exactly as it had before, the same strange light barely visible. Lyle took a deep breath, placed his finger on the trigger, and let himself slide off the chair.

"Stop! Don't m—"

"Shut up." Lyle raised the pistol and aimed it at the paper bag over the figure's head. They stood at the same point in the cavern, their feet lined up precisely. "I know who you are." Lyle pulled his own paper Yumm Burger bag from his pocket and threw it on the ground.

The figure leaned down to remove his own bag.

"No. Leave it on." Lyle's voice wavered crazily, and his breathing was heavy. The figure lifted his head and lowered his hands.

"You caused all of this. You threw everything off. But I'm going to end it and then I'm going to raise my hands and leave." Lyle sobbed now. "None of this should have happened, but it did. Now I'm going to make sure that it never happens again." His hand trembled as though it was straining to hold some enormous weight.

"Then you are stronger than I am," the figure said softly.

Two seconds later a deafening report of pistol fire echoed through the cavern. The figure fell to the ground.

Lyle felt dizzy. The cavern around him spun and teetered. *Don't move. Don't step.* Lyle leaned forward and closed his eyes tightly. He heard something, a sound like a leaky faucet. He opened his eyes and saw something dripping from his head. Blood.

His trembling fingers reached up and touched his forehead. There was a hole, a perfect circle of a hole, right through his forehead. Lyle teetered to the left and fell toward the open end of the cavern. This movement brought the first touches of pain and the blood from the hole began to flow a little more. Lyle's mind felt as though it were melting, oozing over everything like magma.

His thoughts were a hazy flurry of images. Tommy. Alice. Nora, her soft lips and thick brown hair. *Tomando açaí com paçoca* with his *avô* in *BH*, the sun shining through the coconut trees and onto the balcony of his apartment. The Nile stock alert. The figure with the bag on his head.

He looked back but a wall had materialized in the space where the figure had been. Lyle looked at the walls of the cavern and on them saw himself staring down at the ground, waiting for the hole to appear.

***

Lyle sat on the ground of the cavern for days. For weeks. For years. For seconds. He could not tell. He deliberated for decades, centuries, millennia, hours maybe about what to do. All the while, he did not move one inch from his spot in the tunnel. All the while the hole remained in his head, unhealed and dripping ever so slightly. The thought crossed his mind that all he had to do to end the loop forever was to step forward and let time impose itself on his wound. It would all be over in seconds.

But Lyle did not want to die. Why should he have to die? It was not his fault, none of this was. Perhaps he was the last Lyle. If he died, no iteration of him would be with Nora, Alice, and Tommy. And so he sat thinking for an immeasurable period of time. It was no time, and it was eternity.

The longer he sat there, the more the walls of the tunnel seemed to melt away into the images of his own mind. Eventually, he could not see the tunnel walls even if he wanted to. Everything was memories. Glimpses of his life crashed upon him like waves in an ocean of dreams. The time Nora dropped his birthday cake which they then made into cake balls. Alice coming home from 1st grade crying because all the short boys that she towered above teased her about her height. Tommy's little hand wrapping itself around Lyle's finger in the delivery room.

These images and countless others flashed themselves across Lyle's mind, but he could only hold them for an instant. His mind was a pinball ceaselessly clinging and clanging and rolling and bouncing off the memory-soaked contours of his consciousness.

***

Centuries later maybe, the image of the downtrodden Lyle avoiding a conversation with Nora about the money he had lost and staring up at a theater screen flashed across his mind's eye. Lyle reached out to that old version of himself.

A hole appeared above him.

Lyle pulled the Yumm Burger bag over his head and stood up.

"Stop!"

ABOUT THE AUTHOR

Stephen Nothum (stephennothum.com) is a fiction writer and learning designer based in Eugene, Oregon. Stephen's work focuses on topics like pop culture, education, perceptions, mental health, social issues, and the concept of reality.

His writing has been featured in HASH Journal, The Bookends Review, Utah English Journal, and Zoetic Press. Stephen has presented at conferences at both state and national levels on writing, writing education, and reading.

Teething and Other Tales from the American Dystopia is Stephen's first book publication, but it will not be his last. To stay up to date on Stephen's work, be sure to visit his website to sign up for the newsletter.

For inquiries, reach out at stephen@stephennothum.com.

Printed in Great Britain
by Amazon

57128813R00148